Grumpy Billionaire Firefighter

An Enemies to Lovers Stuck Together Romance

Willow Finn

Copyright 2023 by Willow Finn - All rights reserved.

In no way is it legal to reproduce, duplicate, or transmit any part of this document in either electronic means or in printed format. Recording of this publication is strictly prohibited and any storage of this document is not allowed unless with written permission from the publisher.

All rights reserved.

Respective authors own all copyrights not held by the publisher.

Contents

1. One: Jesse — 1
2. Two: Jade — 9
3. Three: Jesse — 17
4. Four: Jade — 24
5. Five: Jesse — 29
6. Six: Jade — 37
7. Seven: Jesse — 45
8. Eight: Jade — 53
9. Nine: Jesse — 61
10. Ten: Jade — 70
11. Eleven: Jesse — 78
12. Twelve: Jade — 85
13. Thirteen: Jesse — 92
14. Fourteen: Jade — 100
15. Fifteen: Jesse — 107
16. Sixteen: Jade — 114
17. Seventeen: Jesse — 121

18. Eighteen: Jade — 127
19. Nineteen: Jesse — 134
20. Twenty: Jade — 141
21. Twenty-One: Jesse — 145
22. Twenty-Two: Jade — 149
23. Twenty-Three: Jesse — 155
24. Twenty-Four: Jade — 160
25. Twenty-Five: Jesse — 165
26. Twenty-Six: Jade — 171

Chapter One

One: Jesse

I pulled the zipper of my bag open to ensure I had everything I'd need: sturdy jeans, some light-colored tee shirts for working, and a good pair of boots. Well, my boots were sitting on the floor in the back of my truck. There were plenty of socks, and everything was set. I'd prepared well, as always, and I knew I wouldn't have to come back home for any forgotten items.

Living a double life of physical labor had left me quite sturdily built, with the arms and stomach to show for all that I had done. Keeping my hair short was only natural because I didn't need it getting in my face when I was trying to pull someone out of a fire, where both my hands were full and I couldn't even get to my hair under my helmet. Or when I was hauling hay for the cattle on my parents' ranch. It was just easier short and out of the way. When I'd started the job, I was amazed at the amount of physical labor required of firefighters. In fact, I could hardly stand after a weekend spent at the ranch and a few days at the fire station, on duty. Not even working outdoors on the ranch every day had prepared me for the physical demands of fighting fires.

Now, that hardly fazed me.

However, that double life also left my home empty most days. That bothered me. Between staying at the fire station on shift and staying at the ranch, I wished someone could stay in the house to let me know it was all right.

My house sat empty more often than not. While I wasn't too worried about robbery because I didn't leave anything of much value there, I knew that there could always be problems with the house. Being a firefighter was a great job. However, it left me feeling empty most days now, especially after some of the things I had experienced on the job. There were people I hadn't saved. Screams I couldn't get out of my head. Smells I never wanted to encounter again.

And, honestly, having someone in the home when I wasn't there sounded like a good use of a beautiful space. It was a great house, and leaving it empty so often was a shame.

Perhaps it would be worth staying home long enough to post an ad online. I'd been thinking of renting out the space, and now felt like the right moment. It was a beautiful, two-story home. The second floor had very little up there, and I was pretty sure I'd never used any of those rooms personally. It was a small floor – just two small rooms and a bathroom – but I had never found a use for them as I was never here long enough to care what they were used for.

I sighed. I didn't know why the urge to post the listing felt so important, but I knew I wasn't quite ready to head to the ranch just yet.

.

I scanned the house, walking from room to room. It was situated in a great spot in Lantana and had a gabled roof and a paved driveway. There were some places that only had gravel driveways, which weren't all that great on tires. If I was going to do this listing right, I had to put up pictures of all the common rooms as well as the private rooms on the top floor. The only thing I didn't want was someone running a business out of my home, as that would bring too many visitors, and I would not be able to get enough sleep on the few nights I actually was home.

Thankfully, I employed a cleaning service to keep the house clean since I had no time to do so. This meant everything was in perfect condition for pictures. I turned on all the lights and started taking pictures on my phone. They weren't perfect, but they would have to do. I didn't have all the fancy photography equipment that a real estate agent would have, but I didn't think I needed it.

I made sure to show it all off. The kitchen got three different photos because it was so large, and I made sure to take one that showed off the gorgeous view into the backyard. This house attracted me precisely because it was close to the fire station I worked at and only a couple of hours away from the ranch.

Everyone else would probably be attracted to the beautiful views outside the windows and the great location. Though it was still a suburb, it wasn't the awfully far-out-there boonies suburbs that were being constructed around Houston these days. It was decently close, making getting to the shopping areas much easier. It was also easy to get out to the other areas that were pretty decent, but I supposed the best pull would be that I would be away for a good bit of the time.

My main job was working at the fire station, and when I was on shift at the station, I often slept there. Considering it was set up to hold multiple people on shift, it wasn't the hardest thing in the world.

I finished taking photos downstairs and went upstairs. The cleaning service had even vacuumed the stairs this week. I should have tipped them more, seeing that. Stairs were some of the hardest things to clean, especially carpeted stairs.

Upstairs, I took pictures of both bedrooms. There was no furniture up here, so getting good, clean photos of the rooms was easy. The bathroom had been the only thing I set up because I had, at one point, thought that I was going to sleep up there. The rooms were nice, and I really liked the layout up here. But it was easier to use the master bedroom downstairs in case I was called in late at night while I was home.

That made it look better for the photos, though.

Once they were all taken, I sat down at my laptop in my room. I emailed all the photos to myself and started to craft a listing for the rental. The upper floor would be completely for the tenant as they saw fit to use, and the only room off-limits would be the master bedroom – which had its own bathroom and large, walk-in closet. So, I was all set as far as not having to share a bathroom.

There was also a half-bath on the main floor for guests so that they didn't have to go into the master bathroom. It had a toilet, a small sink, and some counter space. In my opinion, it was a great set-up.

"There we go. It looks pretty professional if I say so myself," I mused when I was done.

It was listed on a site known for hosting rental ads, though I saw that most of the other ads were put up by rental management agencies or landlords who had multiple properties. The only other difference between my ad and theirs was that I was advertising for about half the price of their rentals. Since I was only leasing the rooms, not the full house, I didn't think they needed to pay much for rent.

Besides, I had taken the utilities spike into consideration so that I could give my tenant a single bill. The idea was to make this as good a deal as possible so that plenty of people would be looking to get the rental. I wanted to have enough options to pick someone who truly needed the cheaper rent and the privacy since I would not be home often.

I supposed it helped that I owned my house outright instead of trying to make a mortgage payment. The only costs they were helping pay were the extra utilities from being home more often, and the rest would go back into the house if they needed maintenance. I had already done some, but I would call a professional to do any for the tenant.

Especially if it was something I didn't feel comfortable trying to figure out in twenty-four hours. Small repairs, like fixing a loose bolt or something, I could do while I was home.

After making sure it had been posted and all the contact information was right, I closed my laptop. My stomach growled. I supposed it was about dinner time, which meant that I needed to get on the road as soon as possible. The ranch gates closed at nine each night, and I didn't want to have to call the main house to open them for me if I arrived late.

Before I left, I received an email stating that my ad had been rejected because I had forgotten to include a few things. The site wanted me to add things like what the deposit was, if the renters needed rental insurance, and why they should rent from a first-time landlord. The email also suggested that if I needed help, plenty of agencies would be more than happy to manage the property for me.

I groaned. This was going to take forever to fix, and I didn't have the patience tonight. However, I knew it had to be done before leaving for the ranch. I decided to order pizza, but before I even continued working on the ad, I double-checked the time.

Since I had gotten off earlier than normal, it was only three in the afternoon. I felt a little stupid now for trying to rush the ad. Perhaps it would be a good idea to slow down and take the next couple of hours to properly research.

Just in case, I called my father.

"Jesse! When are you heading to the ranch? I thought you'd be here by now. You're off the next three days, right?"

"Yeah, I am," I replied with a sigh. "I'm having a little bit of technical trouble before I leave. Would you be willing to wait a little longer for me tonight if I can't leave before seven?"

"What kind of technical trouble? Are you all right, Jesse?" my father asked, and I could hear the worry in his voice.

Same old Dad. At least I didn't have to worry about him ever not worrying that I was going to make it home safely after a shift at the firehouse. Though I suspected he was more upset that I was not going to be there on time, I knew that he was probably going to find a way to be all right with it.

"I'm trying to post an ad to rent out the top floor of the house, but I'm getting tripped up with details," I replied. "I should have been more careful the first time, but I'm going to try to finish this before heading over."

"I can wait up," he said before I'd even asked. "I'll see you when you get here. Text me when you finally leave Lantana, Jesse. I want to know an ETA so I can open the gate for you. Don't worry about being late, I can keep myself busy. I have a few things I've been putting off doing anyway."

After taking a deep breath and making some adjustments, I started filling out the ad. Again. I decided to change up some of the wording, too, since the original wording had only been the first thing that came to mind.

First, I made sure the issues that had popped up the first time were filled in this time. This included that I would prefer that those who were going to rent from me had renter's insurance and that the deposit would be half a month's rent to cover any cleaning expenses when they moved out beyond typical wear and tear of items that would already be covered as part of my duty as their landlord.

As for why someone should rent from a first-time landlord, I decided I would be honest. I wrote in this area that it was a shame this house sat empty most nights, and I'd like someone else to be able to enjoy the house as much as I do when I'm home. While a first-time landlord, I also noted that by my being gone most of the time, I would give the tenant almost as much privacy as if they were renting from a more experienced landlord or management company.

Once these areas were filled in, I cracked my knuckles softly. The rest of this was going to be child's play, but I wanted to make the property look appealing to any potential renters. I listed around half of the rent in the area because I could afford that. Again, I noted that this included utilities.

That was incredibly rare to find in Lantana. A quick search on the site confirmed that I was practically the only rental to include utilities in the price of the rent. Most landlords were looking to cover various costs and make a profit on the rent from their tenants. Honestly, I didn't need to make any money from this; I just wanted someone to enjoy the house and keep it from looking abandoned most days.

"Hmm. What else should I share in this ad?" I pursed my lips.

This ad needed to be well put together. If it wasn't well-written, I wouldn't attract renters.

I decided to write up a generic overview of the house, with the only caveat being that I didn't want anyone in the master bedroom. The rest of the house was theirs to explore, and this rent included exclusive use of the two bedrooms and full bathroom upstairs.

I supposed this set-up would be good for a mother with up to two children, but it would also be good for friends who were looking to move in together. Or one person who could afford the rent and wanted an extra room for a home office of sorts.

Thinking about the home office made me put a few restrictions on the "upstairs is yours to do whatever you want with" phrasing. I didn't want a business being run out of my home. They could work from home – including meeting with clients or coworkers over video chat – but I would not allow anyone to run a business out of my home and conduct most of their business out of the living room.

Once I was done with the ad, I submitted it. As I waited for it to get approved, I grabbed a few things that I decided I would take to the ranch with me at the last minute. Once those were in the truck, I looked at the laptop again.

This time, the ad had gone through. That was wonderful. I shut my laptop down and put it back in my room. As much as I knew that I *could* leave it in the dining room for now, I didn't want to. Everything had a place, and I thought it needed to stay that way. Especially if someone else was going to be moving into the house and staying there when I wasn't around.

I called my father back and let him know that I was on my way. I didn't think that I would be late enough he had to worry about opening the gate for me, but I appreciated that he had been willing to do that.

Chapter Two

Two: Jade

I stared at the phone with my lips pursed. A bracelet had completely fallen apart in front of me, and the beads were now scattered around the apartment floor.

"Is that the sound I think I just heard? The sound of beads on the floor?" The other side of the line crackled a little as Maria spoke.

I pushed my long black hair out of my face, frustrated that I didn't put it in a braid. Perhaps now I should, but that was a moot point since the beads were already rolling away from me.

"Yeah. At least my arms will fit under the couch. A few of them fell under there. I think I lost my grip on the bracelet or the pin on my pants came undone. That just came undone out of *nowhere*," I lamented. "Hold on. I need to clean up the beads before I lose any of them."

"I understand."

The line went quiet as Maria patiently waited for me to gather all the beads from the floor. The last thing I needed was to step on a bead and break it. These beads took forever to get to me, and the next shipment wouldn't be for a while. I wanted to use all the beads first. Or, most of them. These beads weren't popular this time of year, either, so it wasn't like I was in a hurry to get the beading finished on this piece.

"All right. I have all the beads, I think," I said as I got up from the floor. "What were we talking about?"

I could hear Maria smiling through her words. "I said I have something important to talk to you about."

"Ah okay. Yeah, I missed that part when the bracelet fell apart."

Maria replied with a soft laugh. "So, you said your jewelry is selling well online, right?"

"Yeah. Surprisingly well. If I wanted to, I could try to go full-time as a jeweler and have my nursing as a backup career if it fails for some reason," I informed my friend. "I just haven't taken the leap. I don't want to do it all on my own. Besides, there's really not much of a demand for it here. They sell *online*. I'm spending quite a bit to send these pieces all over the US, ensuring they don't fall apart because, well, the bracelets are great, but the post office isn't exactly known for being gentle with their packages. And all the beads are glass, so it takes some doing to make sure they're packed safely and shipped properly." I shook my head. "Why do you ask?"

"I'm thinking of renting shop space in town. There's an opening in a cute downtown area, and I think I can afford it," Maria said. "I think it'd be a good idea to have a multitude of things that people can pick from. While I do quite a bit of crafting already – and think I'd be selling beaded curtains, bags, and belts – I don't do jewelry. That's your area of expertise. And if we went in on it together..." She trailed off, the suggestion clear.

"In Lantana? There's a shop opening in Lantana that would have space for us?" I furrowed my brows.

That didn't seem likely. I had visited Maria a couple of times after we had graduated from nursing school and found Lantana to be an interesting area north of Houston. However, the smaller shops all appeared to have been multi-generational family-owned shops. How had one gone out of business?

"Yeah. It's got a perfect window to show off the beaded curtains and some other crafts we want to sell. Jade, I think it'd be a fun opportunity for the both of us," Maria continued.

I considered for a few seconds. I could hear Maria holding her breath on the other end.

Honestly, it might work. I'd wanted to try selling in person, and I really wanted a break from full-time nursing. So many pieces were falling into place.

"I just have one small question," I said finally. "Where would I live if I decided that is where I wanted to be right now?" I pursed my lips. "Last I checked, you're living in a one-bedroom apartment, right? You have no space for another person to come stay for an extended period of time with a whole house-full of their own things."

"You're right about that," Maria said. "However, I think there are plenty of rentals around, or if you're interested in owning your own house, you could always look at what's on the market. It might take some time, but I'd love to see what we could do together."

"What are you going to do if this falls through, Maria?" I couldn't stop myself from asking.

While I already had a backup plan, I wanted to be sure that Maria would also be all right if this didn't work out. Sometimes, businesses failed in their infancy. It was just part of being a business owner. We both had to take that risk.

"Same as you, honestly. There are plenty of hospitals around here that could use an extra nurse or two, and I'm sure that they'd be willing to take us on quickly if it came to that," Maria said. "Look, I know it's a huge ask, and so sudden. But I think it'd be a fun thing to do. We always joked about it in nursing school. Why keep it a joke when we have the chance to make it a reality?"

"Could I sign the lease for the building virtually? I'll need a bit of time to give my notice."

I was being swayed already, though I had to admit that going full-time into jewelry had been a pipe dream of mine since I was a child. Having a chance to try so soon after getting out of nursing school and knowing that I could return to online-only selling if I needed to for the success of my brand made me feel like it was worth a shot. Especially if Maria was going to be working in the store with me.

"I'm not sure, but I'm meeting with someone about it in a week. I know it's quick, but the sooner you can get out here, the better, I'd say. I know that means you'll have to break your lease, but I only found out about the shop space being available today. I set up the meeting and immediately realized you would also be a good fit for the shop."

"Well, I appreciate that you kept me in mind, Maria," I replied as I started to put the bracelet back together.

Thankfully, I had done this particular design a thousand times before. These beads were simply small. Or maybe my hands were a little less steady than usual. The thought of having an actual storefront—an actual business—had always felt like a total dream. Now here it was, walking into my life in a five-minute phone call.

"What do you say?"

I couldn't stop myself from grinning in spite of the practical worries in the back of my mind.

"I think we've got to do this! I've got to start looking for a place to live in Lantana and thinking about how I'm going to get everything out there," I said. "This sounds like a wonderful opportunity. I'm excited. And it'll give us an excuse to have more in-person meetings again. I miss going to a coffee shop and just chatting with you. It was always a good way to wind down after a long shift."

"And give us the energy to get our groceries," Maria chipped in.

I laughed a little.

"Yes. That too." Both Maria and I were all too familiar with the exhaustion from working a ten-hour shift, only to realize we didn't have food at home. Starting our own business would mean a whole different rhythm—a whole new way of life for both of us. "I'll start looking into stuff right away. Or," I corrected myself, "as soon as I finish this bracelet. I'll keep you updated, and you tell me all about the building when you find out more."

"Of course, Jade. Let me know what you find, and I'll see what I can do to help you find a place. With the housing market the way it is today, I'm not sure what the rental pricing will be like or what kind of mortgage you'd be able to qualify for," Maria said. "But that's all something we can talk about later. I hope you have a wonderful, uneventful night."

"You too. Have a good shift tomorrow."

With that, we hung up the phone.

I gently set the bracelet on the table in front of me before taping the edges down. Then, I examined all the beads that had dropped to the floor. Only one had some paint scrapping, but that was easy enough to fix. I kept extra paint around for a reason. I even had a brush small enough to get into the bead to fix it.

Once the paint had been fixed, I decided now was as good a time as any to start getting ready for bed. I had an early shift tomorrow and didn't want to be late.

After a quick shower, I took a moment to admire my long dark hair and hazel eyes. Some would have said my build was too fit and slim for them, but I liked it.

I had worked hard to maintain the muscles from my sports days in nursing school, and it didn't hurt that some areas of nursing required my strength if there were no lifts available to help get patients into a wheelchair or into the beds from a wheelchair. My muscles allowed me to take some of the slimmer patients and do those transitions easily. Larger patients took some extra time, and sometimes another set of hands, but I was proud to be able to treat them with respect and dignity.

Everyone deserved that, no matter their circumstances.

I finished drying my hair and headed to the bedroom. Instead of immediately going to bed, I double-checked that my alarms were set. I needed to be up at three in the morning to get ready and leave on time for a five a.m. clock-in. I typically swung through McDonalds for coffee on my way in. Mornings had never been my favorite, but hot coffee definitely helped.

I'd asked for night shifts, as I was a night owl in college. I supposed this was as close as they were able to get me to that, but I needed plenty of sleep now I was no longer in an atmosphere that encouraged people to stay up all night long to study, party, and get everything done.

Having patients depend on me for the right dosages of medications meant my sleep was now sacred to me. I needed to be alert during my shift, and I couldn't do that properly if I was drowsy. I had started thinking about it that way in my second year of nursing school, and so far, it hadn't steered me wrong.

I spent about a half hour on my phone browsing rentals and houses on the market in Lantana just to see what the prices were looking like. I had some savings put away since I had no energy to do anything but bead and send stuff out en masse when I finished a shift. I figured I could live off my savings for about a year if I planned it right, but I would have to be incredibly careful with how much I was spending on the roof over my head.

This was certainly not a problem that would be solved tonight, but depending on how much the business lease would come to once it was split between myself and Maria, I was pretty sure I'd have to rent a home or apartment instead of buying something outright. Either way, as long as I could set up a room to bead in where no one would disrupt me, I would be happy.

It'd be better than trying to bead in the living room and risking all the glass beads I used getting busted on the floor and having to order more.

Before I turned off my lamp, I opened up one more rental site to check it for affordable apartments in Lantana.

Just to see if moving would really be feasible.

As expected, most apartments were tiny and super expensive. But on the third page of listings, I saw one that was different.

A whole floor of a house rented for *way* below market value.

The online listing looked incredibly promising. It was a beautiful home in the northern portion of the neighborhood. The house had a beautiful backyard, and the listing even said that rent included utilities. That was something rare to find outside of college towns, especially considering the prices of utilities were rising these days. If I rented for a price like that, I could save money to eventually buy a house of my own, and budgeting would be even easier since I'd only need to keep track of five different bills: my rent, my groceries, my cell phone bill, my credit card, and my portion of the lease for the store that Maria and I were going to be opening.

Furthermore, the listing stated that the entirety of the house would be mine to use as I pleased – minus the master bedroom. With so much space, I wouldn't need to worry about having enough space for my things—not even all of my beading supplies.

Before plugging in my phone to charge, I texted a link to Maria. *Look at this place! How is this real?!*

She replied in seconds.

Message the landlord NOW.

I smiled. I needed to sleep, but it wouldn't take long to fill out the short information request form on the website that would be sent to the landlord. I submitted my info, gave my phone number, and closed the browser.

I put my phone on the nightstand and turned off the lights. It was all a dream for now, but that dream would soon be a reality. And that was always the best feeling in the world.

I couldn't help smiling as I fell asleep.

Chapter Three

Three: Jesse

Three days later, when I returned home from the ranch, I took a shower. The lifestyle at the ranch left me sweaty more often than not, and though I often showered there, a shower once I got home always felt amazing.

Having the rest of the afternoon and evening before I had to be anywhere, I decided it was time to see if anyone had responded to the ad I had put up. My phone hadn't been ringing, but the site also let potential tenants email for more information. Since I hadn't been checking that either when I was at the ranch, it was possible I had plenty of bites coming in.

Once my laptop was fully booted up, I pulled up my email. It was just as empty as it had been before I left for the ranch with the exception of a single new email. I clicked on it and found that it was someone emailing about the listing. Their information was sparse, and I realized they must have used the online form instead of emailing me directly.

The crickets singing their hymns in the wake of my ad left me discontented. How could people be so stupid to pass up such a great rent price for all that was included? I even had a fire pit outside that was in great condition.

I'd expected far more people to be interested in my ad.

I returned to my ad to see if I could figure out what had happened. Except, this time, instead of logging into the landlord portal, I visited as someone who was interested in renting. There was a link to fill out applications, and I quickly realized that I hadn't put together a proper application that people could submit online. And there was no way to fix that without taking the listing down.

I heaved a sigh.

"Great. That's just great. It'd be *wonderful* if this site would tell you everything you had to do before you press submit instead of allowing you to submit half an ad with no application," I muttered. "What am I going to do now?"

If I took down the ad and put it up again with the proper application, would I get more bites? Or was it going to be a waste of time? How much did I need a pool of interested applicants to pick from? Was one query really going to be enough? What if they'd already found somewhere else to live in the three days while I was at the ranch?

I pursed my lips. Decisions, decisions.

I decided to keep the ad up. Instead of using the application process on the website, the fact that those who were truly interested would have to make more of an effort to get ahold of me would tell me who was truly interested in this place and who was just poking around to see what they could find in a price range they could afford.

Or at least, that's what I told myself to feel better about missing the "application" section of the posting. I just hoped and prayed that the right person would find their way to the ad.

I was a little disgruntled that this person had only used the form. Somehow, I'd expected to be called directly since I'd listed my phone number. It seemed odd to just click "send" on a form when you were applying to share someone's house. It felt weird, and I didn't like it. Sure, the person had submitted their own email and phone number, but it still felt impersonal and shifty.

"People are stupid to pass up this well-priced rental because they don't want to go the extra step to email or call," I muttered.

I emailed the lone interested party back with a thanks for their interest, and a few times when we could talk on the phone about details. I saw on the application that they were out of town so I figured offering a tour wasn't an option.

After that was done, I took a deep breath.

I had all afternoon to do anything I wished. And after the hard work I'd done at the ranch, some pizza sounded great. I ordered a plain cheese pizza to the house, then settled in to watch the news for a little while as I waited for something more to happen.

By the time the newscast had ended, I had finished my pizza and cleaned up the scraps. I put the leftovers in the fridge. Those would be good for breakfast before I left for the station tomorrow morning.

Unfortunately, there was no inkling that anyone else was interested in the rental by the time I was getting ready to go to bed. Perhaps that was for the best. I had started thinking about how I would have handled going through a large number of applications and realized that I was nowhere near equipped to deal with talking to that many people to let them know that I had already rented the unit out when I found a tenant.

Or even to send that many emails out.

I was far more equipped to spend my days in solitude, away from the large cities. Though I only lived here to make my commute and life easier when working at the fire station, I preferred the situation at the ranch. Most others would probably prefer the situation here in

Lantana, which is why I had first started thinking about renting out the upper floor of the house to someone else.

I shook my head. That might have been the reason I wasn't getting any interest in the property, and not the broken application process.

The next morning, I woke up naturally to get up and get ready for my shift. I had to be there by nine, so waking up at seven was fine. It gave me two hours to get ready and to the station.

After making sure I hadn't missed a message, I heated up the leftover pizza from last night and got ready for the day at the station.

Just after I walked into the station, my phone rang. It was from out-of-town. I figured it was probably the only renter who was interested in what I had to offer in Lantana. Her voice did not quite match what I thought it would be, though I supposed I didn't have much to base my assumptions on. All I knew is that she had some nerve calling me an hour before I'd said I'd be available today.

"Hello? This is Jade Santana. I emailed you about your rental?"

I hadn't realized I had zoned out.

"I'm still here. Yes, this is Mr. Delaney," I replied. "Are there any questions you have that were not answered in the listing, Miss Santana?"

I quietly hoped that this was not her backing out. Her voice quivered as she said 'hello' earlier, and I hoped it was just because she was nervous. If she backed out, I would have to pull this ad off the internet and start again, making sure that I went through the process with a fine-toothed comb.

I did not want to take the time to list this again. The process was arduous as it was; to have to do it again and do *more* would have been pointless, in my opinion. People were already looking elsewhere, and I didn't know why. Until I knew that, perhaps it was best not to relist my ad.

"No, no," Miss Santana said. "I was just curious about move-in availability and the application process. I, well," her voice hesitated on the other end of the line. "Well, I have a great work opportunity, but it means moving to Lantana as quickly as possible..."

I frowned. "As quickly as possible? As in...?" I waited for her to elaborate.

"Would Wednesday work?"

I blinked in surprise. Now that her voice had evened out, it sounded quite chipper and ready for the move. However, asking me if she could move in *earlier* than the end of the week was bold.

"Wednesday, you say?" I repeated her question, just to make sure that I understood her properly.

"Yes. Provided my application is approved," she added hastily.

I pursed my lips.

"Let me check my schedule," I said before putting myself on mute so that I could check my calendar.

I let out a deep sigh.

If that was her only request, I suppose I could meet it. So far, she was still my only option, and she sounded completely polite, too.

I took my phone off mute and put it to my ear again.

"I can make Wednesday work," I replied. "What time do you think you'll get to the house on Wednesday?"

"Well... let's see here..."

I could hear her thinking out loud.

"The GPS says that it's going to be at least a three-hour drive from where I currently live," her voice got louder again as she turned her attention back to me, "So say noon? I figure I'll have at least an extra hour of traffic, stops, etc. in there somewhere," Miss Santana said. "Probably three in the afternoon at the absolute latest. Oh wait!"

I waited for her to continue. An awkward silence fell on the line.

"Oh my gosh, I just realized we're in different time zones. Which means, I'll be there at two your time. And I also just realized I also messed up when you said to call. I'm so sorry about that. Is now an okay time?"

I tried to contain a sigh. She was polite, but I didn't like her scatterbrained way of doing business. I scowled but chose to return to her previous question.

"Wednesday at two works for me. I look forward to meeting you, Miss Santana."

"Jade, please," she said. "After all, we'll be living in the same house – even if the ad says that you're not going to be home all that often."

I could almost hear the smile in her voice. Something about how cheery she was caught me off-guard. Most people, me included, hated moving. The last time I moved, it had purely been so that I could pursue my passion for fighting fires and saving people. Most of the fires I fought had been set on purpose in a fireplace or a firepit and got out of hand or were accidental. I didn't see many arson fires, and I was perfectly all right with that.

I'd been fighting long enough to know how awful arson fires were compared to anything else.

"All right... Jade," I said. "I'll see you on Wednesday, then. Will you need any help unloading your moving truck or will you be able to handle it all?"

"I should be able to handle it. I'm going to be packing it up on my own," she revealed. "If I can't pack it on my own, then I'll be sure to take you up on that offer. Sound good?"

"Sounds like a plan to me. I'll text you if I have any more questions about the lease agreement before emailing it to you."

I kept my voice as even and neutral as possible.

We ended the conversation a few minutes later, thankfully. As I put my phone back in my pocket, I sighed deeply.

I supposed the only thing left to do was to make sure the house was ready for her to move in. I pulled my phone back out of my pocket.

"Quick Maid's Clean Up. Lucy speaking," the voice on the other end of the call answered when the call went through. "How can I help you today?"

"My name is Jesse Delaney. I'm calling to see if I scheduled any cleaning for my house in Lantana this week," I said.

I heard a few clicks on the other end. It sounded like Lucy was looking me up in their system.

"No, there is nothing on the calendar this week for your house, Mr. Delaney," Lucy replied. "Would you like to change that?"

"Is there any chance you have a cancellation tomorrow?" I didn't want to take any chances and have the cleaners arrive while we were there, moving Jade in. "I have someone moving in with me later this week, and I would like the place to be clean before she arrives on Wednesday."

After a few minutes, I was on their schedule for tomorrow. I hung up the call and took a deep breath. With that, there was nothing more I could do until it was time for my tenant to move in I looked around the station. It was a slow day and there were plenty of us here. I could call my Dad and share the good news.

I'd also have to get another key cut for Jade. That could be taken care of on the way home since there was a home improvement store just a few minutes away from the main exit I'd be taking to get home.

Chapter Four

Four: Jade

My phone buzzed at me while I was on my lunch break.

"Oh! It's the number from the listing," I muttered as I opened my phone.

Jesse Delaney at your service. Finalizing the lease agreement. I'll send it over asap.

It was a short, sweet text. To the point. I appreciated that. I figured I should see if he needed any other information from me before sending the contract.

Do you want to run a credit or income check?

As I ate my sandwich and waited for Jesse Delaney to respond, I pulled up my current lease. My current work had been super flexible when I told them I wanted to move, and they hadn't even insisted on working my final two weeks. My supervisor told me that my resignation actually came at a super convenient time when they were taking on new staff and entering a slower month where fewer surgeries and appointments had been scheduled.

However, I still needed to tell my current landlord that I would be leaving. I hadn't wanted to do that until I found a place in Lantana, but now that was all taken care of, I had to give notice that I intended to vacate my lease and pay any remaining rent for the month. Thankfully, I was on a month-to-month rent.

Another buzz pulled me out of searching for the information I needed. I checked my phone.

No. Month-to-month or 12 month? Could do something in-between if that's better?

I smiled. I took this as final confirmation that I had gotten the rental, which was wonderful. If I could make it to the meeting with Maria, then there would be no reason for me to worry about how much the rent on the building would be.

Is there a price difference?

Now, I took a good look at my contract. It appeared all I needed to do was pay any rent left for the month – which there wasn't since I had gotten in the habit of paying my rent in full when it was due, despite there being payment plans – and write up a notice of intent to vacate the apartment and take it into the management office. They could start showing the apartment as soon as I was out of there, or as soon as the contract was up.

Whichever happened to come first.

No. So I guess month-to-month makes sense.

Mr. Delaney seemed pretty new to the rental market, but the next few texts with him were all about the rental process and what he was expecting. He was more than happy to let me pay until I needed to leave so long as I gave him notice. That sounded great to me.

It was exactly the same situation as what was going on here. Except a bit more personal.

After making sure Mr. Delaney didn't have any other questions, I started typing up a letter of intent to vacate. I had never had to write up one of these before, as my other leases had all had a definitive end date. Then again, that was the case usually with student housing. As soon as the semester was up, or the year, one moved or renewed the lease.

Once I had the text telling me that Mr. Delaney had sent me the new rental agreement, I put my vacate notice on hold for a while. I wanted to get a good look at the rental agreement and see what he had put together.

It was a crude PDF file that I was supposed to print out, fill out, and then scan in and email back to him. It was becoming increasingly common for people my age to not own printers. However, thanks to my beading business, mine was up and running so I could easily print out shipping invoices and other labels.

The moment I got home from work, I printed the lease, and got to work filling in the rental agreement.

It was a pretty rough agreement, hitting all the legal marks without much fanfare. It laid out the terms of the rental, the rent that I'd be paying, and what that rent entitled me to. It also stated that the deposit was due before moving in, which I had expected. I could afford that. And once the deposit from this place was returned, I would be able to put that into my savings or towards some of the other expenses that came with moving out.

I finished filling in the rental agreement, signed it, scanned it, and returned it to Mr. Delaney. He didn't respond right away. That shouldn't have surprised me—I'm assuming he worked a job—but I definitely was curious. I'd be sharing a house with this man. I'd have to know his schedule at some point—if not because he told me, but because I had simply observed his movements as the days went on. I'd always fancied myself a bit of a people-reader. Almost a detective. I enjoyed being able to know what people needed without them asking for it, and in the same way, I liked being able to figure out details of someone's life simply by the clothes they wore or the books they read.

"All right. Where was I with my notice to vacate?" I muttered as I turned my attention back to finishing up the details that were needed to make the move as smooth as possible.

As I glanced over what I'd drafted, I thought about what I knew about my new landlord. From what I had figured out so far, he wasn't much of a people person. He appeared to prefer email and text over being called, but that could also be because of his job— whatever it was. I wondered what he did for a living and what kind of people he invited around the house.

Then again, the ad had said that the landlord was hardly home and that he thought it a tragedy that no one got to use the house while he was away because it's beautiful.

I pursed my lips as I continued to write up the notice.

As much as I wanted to take this rental on blind faith that Mr. Delaney wasn't some kind of creep, I decided that I should look him up to double check. People often say that someone's voice is a good indication of what they're like in their everyday life. He'd sounded nice on the phone, but I was already running his name through various database searches.

While most people just look at someone's social media, I prefer to check the 'lists.' You can't really tell much about someone through their fishing photos, but if they've ended up registered on one of the public criminal databases, then you actually know something.

None of my searches turned up any results. I pulled up a final page where I typed in his name for a rudimentary background check.

No results.

I didn't see myself as a particularly paranoid or nosy person, but it never hurts to be safe. If there was anything else to worry about, then I'd worry about it in Lantana.

Besides, if push came to shove, I hadn't signed a long-term lease that would keep me locked in for a year. There was always an advantage to that.

My phone buzzed.

Got it. Thanks. See you Wednesday.

Chapter Five

Five: Jesse

Wednesday morning finally came, and I got up for breakfast. I'd slept at the fire station since I had an overnight shift. Me and my buddies ate around six in the morning most days here, and I was glad for that. That'd give me plenty of time to get out to the house and get everything I didn't want Jade to see into my room before she arrived.

It wasn't like there were things I was trying to hide. I just didn't want her to see any of the last little messes I'd left around the house.

"You look like you're in a hurry, Jesse," my coworker said. "What's got you in such a rush this morning? Something happen at home? Need to fill in for a friend at one of the other stations around here?"

"I've gotten a renter for the top floor of my home," I said.

It was best not to mince words; the sooner we got the questions over, the better. Once I mentioned it was a young woman moving in, my friend was intrigued but quickly asked for clarification. She was just a renter to me. Nothing more. I made sure everyone knew that.

"Well, I'm glad to see that you're doing something with that house," he said. "It's a beautiful one. Other than hosting get-togethers outside the ranch, I don't know what else you'd use it for. And you're hardly home enough to even host a get-together."

I nodded. That was the whole reason I'd decided to rent out my top floor, after all.

"Well, I should be leaving after breakfast because I have a few errands to take care of before she arrives," I said. "She's got a bit of a drive, so it's going to be an interesting day. If you need me, you know how to reach me."

Those at the table nodded.

"We'll be fine here, but we'll let you know if there's an emergency. Hope moving in your tenant goes well!"

"Good to hear. Thanks."

I took a deep breath as I grabbed my boots and started pulling them on. Thankfully, after living as a firefighter for so long, I had developed a habit of leaving any laced shoes – whether they were my boots or regular sneakers – with the laces undone and loosened so that I could pull them on, tighten them quickly, and get going to what I needed to be doing.

Upon arriving at my truck, I heard my phone buzz.

Just left my apartment. See you this afternoon!

The text came from Miss Santana. I took a deep breath. This was really happening.

I hadn't anticipated feeling all these emotions about renting out the top floor of my house, but I supposed any change to what I considered normal would make me feel this way. The most concerning feeling was that I was actually *nervous* to meet this young woman. Perhaps it was because she was a woman or because I didn't know her all that well. Whatever the case, I pushed all those feelings aside and started towards the house.

Before she arrived, I wanted to be sure that it was clean and that anything I didn't want her seeing was away in the master bedroom or one of the adjoining rooms. The cleaning crew had done a good job yesterday, but I'd left a basket of laundry in the living room and a few other items I needed to tidy up.

I scooped up a couple of sketches of a new fence for the ranch and my work gear. The gear, I stored in the closet near the door. Most of my uniform stayed at the station, but we all kept emergency gear at our homes just in case. I'd taken mine out to clean, but now I hung it carefully back in the hall closet.

In the closet, there were also a few jackets. Since there wasn't usually much of a winter in Lantana, I doubted Jade would need much space for heavy, thick coats, which was good. There was definitely space for a few light jackets, though.

Once all of that was taken care of, I poked through the kitchen. I decided to make a quick run to the grocery store so that the fridge was stocked with at least bread, jams, eggs, that kind of thing. I figured it would be helpful for her if she had a few essentials already in the fridge that she could use to cook tonight and wait until tomorrow to go grocery shopping if need be.

Come one that afternoon, I was convinced that I had everything ready. I'd walked through the upstairs just to make sure everything was ready. The cleaners had done a beautiful job – as always. The top floor sparkled; it was that clean. I put away the few groceries that needed to be put away in the fridge and the freezer—as I had decided to get some frozen ravioli for myself to eat tonight—and then waited.

An hour or so passed before I heard the telltale sounds of someone pulling up and stopping in front of the house.

A quick glance out the window revealed that it was indeed a young woman. She looked down at a phone in her hand, the other shielding the screen. I wondered if there was some reason she could not turn her brightness up even more or if the brightest setting just wasn't enough for her to be able to see it all in this light.

I opened the front door and stepped out to greet her.

"Mr. Delaney?"

"Jesse," I said. "You must be Jade Santana. A pleasure to meet you."

I put on my best smile for her. The last thing that I wanted her to think right now was that she had made a mistake.

"And you. You can call me Jade."

She offered me a smile in return and then quickly opened the back of the rental moving truck she had driven.

"So, I could hardly get everything all packed last night. I think it's good that you're here to meet me... would you mind helping me unload? There are just a few heavy boxes that might be tricky for me to carry up the stairs."

I nodded slowly.

I had indeed offered to help her move everything inside. What kind of a landlord would I be if I had no intentions of fulfilling that promise if she asked me to do so?

She motioned towards the back of the truck.

"Have anything fragile in here?"

"I marked all of that with red masking tape," Jade replied. "All the fragile stuff, I'd like upstairs if you can manage to help me do that."

I nodded slowly.

I suspected she had some knick-knacks or something that she wanted to display, and the fact that she wanted them all upstairs told me that she wanted to display them for herself or her friends. I didn't know yet. Not that it really mattered. I wouldn't be home much to see who she was bringing around.

I grabbed one of the first boxes from the truck and took it inside. She'd labeled some of the boxes "bedroom" or "office" but the unlabeled ones, I just dumped in the living room. Jade seemed to be on top of grabbing most of the fragile items before I could grab them.

From the shape of the box and the weight, I wondered if I had happened to grab her computer. I wondered what she would need a proper desktop for, but it was none of my business.

Once the truck was emptied, she took a seat on the couch. I sat down on one of the chairs in the living room.

"Thank you for your help, Jesse," she said with a soft smile. "My friend was not able to get this afternoon off to help me. So... what is this room supposed to be? When it's not full of boxes?"

I blinked once and then took a deep breath. I wondered if she was going to be this inquisitive the entire time we lived together. However, the one saving grace was that I'd be home perhaps once a week to share the house with her. If that.

"This is usually the living room," I answered. It seemed obvious to me. I mean, there were couches and a TV. Maybe she was just trying to make conversation. I was very new at this whole "landlord" thing, so I wasn't really sure if it was normal to sit chatting with your tenant over a pile of boxes.

"Oh nice! I like it!" She pointed to a painting over the fireplace that depicted my family's ranch. "That's cool."

I nodded. "How about I show you around the house and then let you start unpacking?"

"Sure!" she said with a widening smile.

I took a deep breath and led her around the house. Her enthusiasm was unexpected. How could someone have so much energy after driving for hours and then unpacking a moving truck?

"You've had the house cleaned since you put it up for rent," she mused as she scanned the mudroom. "I wondered why there was a bit of a spot in here. Is it often you come in through here? Does this door lock with a key too?"

"It locks with the regular house key, but I only come through here if I'm coming back from a fire and need to strip off all my gear. The laundry room is through that door," I said, pointing, "and I can easily get some clean clothes. If you ever see a pile of freshly cleaned folded pajamas that aren't going anywhere, that's the purpose they serve," I informed her. "Oh, and while we're on the subject of things that go on around the house, I have one little rule that I'd like you to follow while you live here. I can abide most visiting and working from home—where you call into the office via phone or video conference. However, the one thing I must ask that you refrain from doing while you live here Is working full-time out of the house and having people coming in and out. I refuse to support that."

Jade stared at me for a second longer than seemed normal..

"Yes. You mentioned that multiple times in your posting. And in your lease agreement."

Did she sound mad? It was a basic rule.

"My friend and I are in the process of setting up a storefront downtown so you have nothing to worry about," she said shortly. "Thank you for the warning. I'm assuming I can at least mail things from here?"

I felt my face turn a little hot. "Of course you can mail things from here," I replied. "I just don't want a ton of customers visiting the house."

This question made me wonder what kind of craft business she ran, but I didn't ask any further questions. Did she sell supplies for others to craft with, or was she selling finished crafts?

"So, firefighting. How long have you been doing that?" Jade changed the subject as we returned to the kitchen so I could grab some water.

"Ten years," I replied tersely. I didn't elaborate, and she must have seen the stiffness in my shoulders.

"Oh, lighten up, Jesse," she said. "We're going to be living together. With me working out of the home or out of the store for much of my business, I think I need to know what to expect out of my roommate, even if he is also my landlord. Just a typical schedule?"

"Well, I'm hardly home," I replied, turning to face her. "You'll have mostly free reign of the house, but on the nights I am home, I cannot guarantee any kind of warning. So, I'd appreciate a head's up if you're planning on being loud or up late with friends. Most nights, I sleep at the fire station."

"Then, why do you have a house?"

"I didn't always sleep at the fire station," I said, refusing to elaborate.

I grabbed a glass from the cabinet and filled it with water from the fridge as I counted to ten mentally. If she insisted on being so knowledgeable about my schedule, then she needed to know that there were things I would not talk about.

"And when you're not at the fire station? I don't believe any firefighter works seven days a week. It's a physically demanding job," she stated.

"I work at a ranch the other days of the week," I replied.

The last thing I wanted to tell her was that this was my family's ranch and that I wasn't technically getting paid for the work I did there. The work was its own reward, as I found animals to be much more interesting than humans most days. The work at the fire station was also rewarding, if more demanding.

When I didn't hear an answer from Jade, I saw her staring expectantly at me as if there was something I was supposed to say.

I didn't say anything, so eventually she took the conversation into her own hands.

"Well, not that it really matters since you won't be here most days, but I run an online business selling jewelry. Trying to turn it into a physical store now," she said. "If that doesn't work out, I'm going to find a job as a nurse at a hospital around here. Hospitals usually need extra nurses."

She sounded a bit short and some of her enthusiasm seemed to have drained. I didn't think I'd done anything to make her mad, but she turned and walked out of the kitchen to start unpacking.

I didn't try to stop her.

Though Jade Santana had infectiously upbeat energy, I found it draining. Perhaps I should have found a person who would also hardly be home to share the house with. It was too late now to change that, though, and I guess that would have defeated the purpose of getting a renter in the first place.

Chapter Six

Six: Jade

After talking to Jesse Delaney for the first time in person, I needed some time to process. He did not seem like a friendly person, and I didn't want to be around it any longer than I had to be. Despite the initial reluctance I had felt about the fact that he was not going to be home often, I now felt that it was for the best. I didn't have to worry about intruding and saying the wrong thing if he wasn't home often.

What in the world had induced a man like that to think that he would get along with a roommate? Or had he done it so that he could keep the house from being targeted by thieves? He clearly didn't want to talk about anything except the fact that he did *not* want a business run out of his house. Why was he so obsessed with that? The odds of that happening seemed pretty low, and his constantly bringing it up almost felt like he was trying to get rid of me.

Obviously if I'd wanted to run a storefront out of his house, I wouldn't have applied. End of story.

Whatever the reason for his unfriendliness, I retreated upstairs to start setting up my bedroom and the room next to it. The rooms both had doors that opened onto a main hallway. Thankfully, the bathroom was not connected to either room. It was more of a bathroom that nestled right between the two rooms with a toilet, a small sink with a small vanity, and a shower stall. It was a beautifully done bathroom.

And it was honestly all that I would need. There was space in the shower to set up my little shower caddy, hanging it over the shower head. That was really all the space I needed because my razor could suction cup to the wall.

The first thing I did was set up my small bed frame. My parents had gotten me a new bed and mattress when I moved out on my own, which was a good thing. It was lightweight but durable—perfect for moving.

Once the bed frame and mattress were all set up, I put away all my clothing, my shoes, etc. The bedroom being unpacked also gave me a chance to think about what I wanted to do about the grump who lived with me. While I could abide by the fact that he didn't want me inviting customers into the home, it had caught me off-guard that he kept mentioning it. .

Then again, he appeared to be a first-time landlord.

I sighed. I really wanted to get along with the person I was about to share a house with, but over the years, I'd discovered that I simply did not like unfriendly people. I could find the patience to deal with just about anyone, but unfriendliness just made me mad.

Once my bedroom was mostly set up—barring a few things that had not yet gotten upstairs—I took a look at the other room. It had good lighting and was about the same size as the bedroom. It looked as though it'd be a wonderful place to set up a little exercise and work room.

After I had finished unrolling my yoga mat and setting up the few things I had for that, I marked out a spot for my beading table over by the window. I think the table had gotten dumped somewhere in the living room. Once I hauled it up, this room would be the perfect space to work and work out.

I pulled the curtains back to see how good the natural light was. It was absolutely gorgeous in the middle of the afternoon, almost the evening.

"This will do beautifully for putting together jewelry," I mused.

Then, I went downstairs to find my beading table.

It had probably ended up in the dining room, where I found Jesse enjoying some ravioli. To be honest, it smelled *delicious*. In all the chaos of the move, I had forgotten to eat lunch. My stomach gurgled loudly, and I felt my cheeks flushing.

"You're more than welcome to anything in the fridge, freezer, or pantry tonight," Jesse said without looking up from his phone.

It might have been my imagination, but it felt like he put extra emphasis on the word *tonight*. It made me bristle a bit, like he expected me to just start stealing his food every day and he wanted to make it clear that I was only welcome to nab a toast with peanut butter *tonight*.

"I figured that it would be easier for you to use something that was already here than worrying about eating out or trying to go grocery shopping today, too," he finished.

"Thank you, Jesse," I tried to chill out. I really was hungry. "Maybe I should eat something before moving my beading table..." I pursed my lips as I surveyed the items that had ended up in the dining room. How had my stuff already ended up all over this house? I couldn't see the beading table amidst the boxes.

I could've sworn I'd hauled it in here...

"Are you looking for something?"

"It's a silver table. It looks like a normal table from the top, but if you were to look at it from the side, the sides have been raised," I explained. "It's for my beading. I need it upstairs."

"That's a table?" He raised an eyebrow. "I thought it was something for the kitchen. I put it in the pantry."

My body froze for a second at that, and I felt my jaw clench. First of all, I was mad that he'd just moved my stuff without asking. Second, food was the one thing that I worked incredibly hard to keep away from my jewelry for *so many reasons*.

Not even his short dark hair, handsome features, and scowl would save him if I found food on the felt surface of the beading table.

"For future reference, while you're home," I started softly, "I'd appreciate it if you kept food away from my beading. One wrong move, and you don't know what might stain the glass beads I use. And the felt will pretty much be ruined from the spill regardless of what it is you've spilled." I paused. "Honestly, I'd just appreciate it if you let me take care of moving my stuff, okay?"

I looked at him, hoping that I had kept my voice even enough so that my anger didn't show through. I needed him to get the message.

He shrugged and nodded.

The level of nonchalance he showed me baffled me. Clearly, he was not looking to treat me as a roommate but as a stranger—despite the fact that we were in fact roommates and that he'd already just moved a piece of my furniture to the *pantry*, of all places.

I pulled my beading table out of the pantry and gave it a good look over. Especially the beading area. I had custom-ordered mine to be made from metal so that I could fold it and move it around the apartment I had previously been in. The top was down, which meant that the felt inside and the whole beading area had stayed protected and untouched.

I gently picked it up and remembered why I had made sure it would roll if needed. Thankfully, I had also remembered to make sure to pick the wheels that locked. It had set me back a pretty penny, and I'd only been able to use it a handful of times so far, but now I had a feeling that it was about to become an investment worth every penny.

"Do you need help getting that upstairs?" Jesse's voice came from the dining room, though there was obviously no enthusiasm behind the offer.

I looked through the doorway to the dining room. He hadn't moved from his bowl of ravioli. Hadn't even looked up from his phone. The fact that he offered was nice, but he could have at least made it look sincere. Or was he afraid that if he made it look like a sincere offer, I would take him up on it, and then he'd really be stuck?

It seemed like his generosity in helping me unload had run out the moment the truck was empty. His offer to help was limited to exactly what he'd said in his initial text and no more. Once my stuff was inside, his part was done.

I was miffed but also impressed. At least I could hold him to his word and know that it was what he meant. After all of the other men in my life who had played games, I appreciated that he was at least an honest grump.

"Nope. I can get it up there myself. I had to pick it up from the office when I originally ordered it and carry it up three flights of stairs. I carried it *down* three flights of stairs to move out, too," I told him. I didn't need his help, and I wanted to make sure he knew it.

Without another word, I lugged the beading table upstairs. I set it up under the window. This would be a fine set up. With an imaginary line down the center of the room, I could easily keep my workout station separate from my beading work. The window would provide good natural lighting during the day for the task, and I could get a small lamp in here to help with nighttime beading.

I pulled my desk up from downstairs as well. It fit perfectly next to my beading table. I needed this to work on sending out packages from my online orders, and it was where my desktop would sit.

The rest of the beading things I wanted were in my room.

I rolled a chest of drawers into the closet in the office and hung some organizer-pockets off the back of the door. The chest of drawers stored all the unopened beads and the large organizers that I didn't need when I was working on a single project. It also held my felt, thread, needles, etc. The bottom drawer was empty, and I made a mental note to pick up more boxes and bubble mailers.

With all the beading mostly in one room now, my bedroom had a little more room for a few more things.

I moved more of the boxes from the living room upstairs and noticed that Jesse was no longer in the dining room. With him out of the way, I seized the opportunity to get some food.

My stomach was gurgling louder, and I wanted to be able to say that I had not forgotten to eat completely today. I knew Maria was going to ask when I saw her tomorrow. Thankfully, earlier today, she'd been able to get the lease squared away for the building we would use as our storefront.

I walked into the kitchen and looked through the pantry, the fridge, and the freezer. It appeared that Jesse was a man of simple foods. Most of what was available could be cooked quickly or thrown in the microwave while he did other things to get ready. Instead of complaining, I decided to just make some scrambled eggs.

I'd pick up groceries for myself tomorrow. Thankfully, Maria would be off, and we could take the truck to the nearest rental place and get it all squared away. The last thing I needed was more charges on my card that I had to worry about.

The scrambled eggs didn't take long and brought Jesse back into the kitchen. I felt my shoulders tense when he walked in.

"How long do you think it's going to take to get all of this unpacked?" he asked without preamble, motioning to the dining room and living room.

"Maybe a day or two. I had to move my entire life down here," I replied. "I'm going as fast as I can, I promise. There are just some things you cannot rush. A woman moving still needs to eat. Still needs to rest." At this point, some of the annoyance was definitely showing in my voice.

He nodded slowly.

"I see."

"Why?"

"Curiosity," he replied. "I have a shift at the fire station starting tomorrow, and I'll probably be gone a full week before you see me again. I'd like to have a living room and dining room by the time I get back."

Considering the posting had emphasized that these were "shared" spaces and that he rarely had guests over, his saying that he wanted those areas cleared by the time he came back seemed... it was hard for me to quite identify.

I guess it made me feel like he still saw the house as *his*. Which, of course, it was his. But it made it sound like I was just visiting—not actually living here.

I bit back these thoughts.

"I think I can make that work, or at least move the boxes upstairs to continue unpacking."

"Or even into the garage would work," he said. "Just leave me enough room to park my truck."

I nodded slowly. This man was an interesting subject, and I didn't know what to make of him quite yet. A grump, yes, but there was something more under the surface. Something waiting to be discovered.

If I could make the most of what little time he'd be home, perhaps he would end up being a good friend by the time I moved out to buy my own house.

I certainly didn't want to be enemies.

Chapter Seven

Seven: Jesse

Though I had been at the firehouse last night, my shift did not start until Thursday. Now that Thursday had arrived, I woke up to my alarm early in the morning. I needed to be at the fire station early enough to catch the rundown from the last crew who had worked, and that meant getting there at six. My alarm went off at four-thirty, giving me an hour and a half to arrive at the fire station. I only needed twenty minutes to get there in the morning traffic.

The rest of the time was to make sure that I had enough to eat and that I was ready for the days I'd be at the station. It also gave me time to pack the bag I took to the ranch. After doing this for years, I knew exactly how much time I'd need each morning, depending on where I'd be working and whether I'd be heading straight to the ranch afterwards or not.

However, this morning, I didn't have the privilege of being as loud as I naturally was. Jade was still asleep upstairs. Ideally, I'd get out this morning without waking her up. I wasn't used to having to think about stuff like that.

I started by making myself some scrambled eggs. The ravioli last night was great, but it was not a food I could eat this early in the morning. Not with how heavy the workload could be. It'd be a better thing to have for lunch or something later. Maybe even at the firehouse if I could get a bag there. Then again, the fire chief was in charge of stocking the fridge, freezer, and pantry there.

I wasn't sure he would want to take up precious space for a pound of ravioli for one person who didn't have a medical need for the food to be on hand.

I took the scrambled eggs off the heat and carefully set the pan on one of the cool burners.

It smelled delicious. I sat down to eat at the raised counter. Unless I was eating and trying to stay out of the way, I didn't really use the dining room. That was more for entertainment purposes than when I was home alone. Jade was welcome to eat wherever she wanted, of course, so long as she didn't make a mess. The general rule of 'you make a mess, you clean it up' applied to both of us, after all.

As I was just about to put my plate in the sink after eating, I heard footsteps coming down the stairs. My heart jumped. For a moment, I worried that someone had gotten in the window up there, but I had to remind myself that my living room and dining room were still full of Jade's things to calm my heart.

"What are you doing up? It isn't even five in the morning," she lamented. "And making such a racket!"

"I'm sorry. I'm trying to be quiet, but I think it will be a week or two before I'm really used to having another person around this early in the morning," I replied. "I'm up this early because I have to be at the fire station by six this morning. You can go back to bed. I'm sorry for waking you up."

She rubbed her eyes, still clearly half-asleep. She was wearing a pair of plaid pajama pants with a gray T-shirt to match the pattern's secondary colors. Her hair was pulled back into a large French braid, which I assumed was to keep it from knotting up in her sleep from what my own mother did to keep her hair from getting tangled.

"Do you always have to get up so early?"

"Only when I'm here between my work at the ranch and at the fire station," I replied as I headed back towards my room. "I'll be quieter."

I heard her footsteps trailing back to the stairs and then up the stairs. Once I didn't hear her any longer, I made the decision that I could wash and re-wear the stuff that was left in my bag from the last time I was up at the ranch and call it good. The I could leave immediately after my shift and I wouldn't need to come home again or make any more noise this morning.

If she wanted to get good sleep, it was imperative that I left the house. And quietly. Thankfully, the door didn't stick or anything. The only noise it would make when I shut it would be to lock it, but that wouldn't be loud enough for her to hear from upstairs. I didn't think so, at least.

I left the house, locking the door behind me to make sure that Jade would at least be safe. But also out of habit. For so many years, I had been the only one here. I'd have to make sure to adjust some of my habits to make sure that I didn't wake Jade up again. Wasn't the hallmark of a good roommate who got up so early the ability for them to get up without waking the others up?

I shook my head. Whatever the case, I could leave now.

After the short drive to the fire station, I parked in one of the spots designated for firefighters on duty. Thankfully, it appeared that despite arriving at least a half hour early, I was going to be able to get a good parking spot. One of the men from the last shift must have had to leave early.

I walked in, and to my surprise, I was immediately ribbed about the woman who had moved in with me.

I bit my tongue. If this shift already knew since I had been here the night before last, then my shift certainly knew by now. Firefighters could be gossipy when they didn't have anything else to do, and it wasn't unusual for the other crews to stop by and make sure those on duty were doing well. If they needed help because someone was out, that was usually how the spot got filled.

In fact, I had been the one to fill the spot simply by asking if they needed help before because I hadn't found a rhythm early in my career here.

***

After a long, overnight shift at the fire station, I was ready to head out to the ranch. I got in my truck and let my muscles relax for a moment. We'd had a horrific fire break out in one of the smaller, newer neighborhoods near Lantana, and it had been just... just awful. I was ready to head out to the ranch and forget about the heat and the screams.

The injured people had been rushed to the hospital. I hoped they were okay. I knew from experience that bad burns were some of the most painful injuries you could have.

I turned to see what was in the back of my truck. To my utter shock, the bag I took to the ranch was not in the back. When Jade had come down early yesterday, I must have forgotten to grab my bag from where it sat in my closet. I had just wanted to get away from the awkwardness of having awoken my new roommate and keep her from getting mad at me.

Then again, I supposed I was a little curt with her. Hadn't meant to be, but it was just my nature. Just because she got the best deal on rent in Lantana didn't mean I had to be happy about the way she conducted herself around me. Simply because we lived in the same house did not mean that we had to be friends, as much as it appeared she wished that was the case.

Groaning, I let my head hit the top of my steering wheel for a moment. If my bag was not in my truck, it was at home. And I'd have to brave whatever Jade had decided to do to make sure that I could get what I needed before going to the ranch.

I took a deep breath. Silently, I prayed that she would be upstairs the entire time I was home so that I could grab what I needed and go before she even realized I had returned.

Unfortunately, since it was now dinner time, there was traffic from everyone going home. The streets were absolutely crowded. Instead of taking just twenty or thirty minutes to get home so that I could grab my bag and head to the ranch tonight, I ended up arriving home about an hour later. A full hour. I made a mental note to text my dad to let him know I'd be delayed tonight.

As I parked in the driveway, I noticed that the second story was completely dark. Instead, the lights from the first floor were on which meant Jade was somewhere downstairs in the common areas. My muscles tensed as I realized there was no way Jade would allow me to leave without conversation now. She was probably making dinner. The mere thought of dinner made my stomach growl, despite a quiet promise to myself to pick something up on the way out to the ranch.

I walked up to the front door and found it unlocked. Not entirely surprising, considering Jade probably ran errands or went out or something. When I walked in, however, I found myself listening to the same kind of pop music that always made me to turn off the radio in the truck. I usually tuned it to a rock station, but there were days it wasn't playing anything I liked, and I sat silently.

The roar of the stand mixer in the kitchen could be heard over the thumping music, and I simply followed the sounds into the kitchen.

There, I found Jade making cookies, it looked like. She had flour, sugar, chocolate chips, vanilla extract, and more out on the counter with my lonely cookie sheet.

"Jesse! I didn't think you'd be home until next week." She washed her hands off quickly and then turned the music down. "Did you forget something? I didn't think you'd be back until..." she trailed off as if she'd forgotten exactly when I said I'd be back.

"Yes." I walked out of the kitchen and into my room.

The bag I wanted was sitting on my bed, exactly where I had left it. I could smell the dirty clothes. Driving with those would be awful. I glanced at the clock beside my bed.

It was now just past seven in the evening, and I had a feeling that it would be too difficult to get anyone to stay up to open the gate for me now. Everyone at home was winding down for the night, and there was a slim chance they would even hear their phones ring over the conversation had at dinner.

I had to be honest with myself. I should just wait to go to the ranch until tomorrow morning.

With a sigh of defeat, I dumped the clothes into the laundry hamper that sat mainly for show in my room. I took a quick shower to wash the smell of smoke and fire off my skin, and then threw in the clothes I had been wearing underneath my firefighter gear.

A small load of laundry was probably prudent at this point.

Once that was going, I noticed that there was stuff in the dryer. Jade had probably started running laundry, and this was the last of it. I hoped.

I returned to the kitchen to find that she had turned the music off. That was an improvement, for sure.

"I'm sorry if the music startled you," Jade said as she continued to dump ingredients—measured carefully—into the mixer. "I didn't think..."

"I forgot something when I left for my shift," I replied gruffly. Her head snapped to look at me, her face wore a frown. I sighed and tried to make an attempt at stereotypical pleasantries. "Have you had dinner?"

"I ordered pizza. You're welcome to the leftovers if you wish," Jade said, motioning to the fridge with her head. "It's a simple cheese pizza. I had a friend over to look at what we wanted to do for our store. She's just as much in shock as I am that I'm only paying this much for rent here, with utilities included."

"She can't move in."

Jade rolled her eyes. I didn't know how I felt about that. It had sounded like a hint that she wanted to add a roommate, but I was not prepared to have *two* Jades living in this house.

"We wouldn't be good roommates, anyway," Jade continued. "So, how was the shift?"

"As good as one can hope it would be," I replied. "I decided to run some laundry before going back to the ranch."

"Oh! I have stuff in the dryer. Let me get that out of your way."

Jade appeared to be a little scatterbrained, just as she had been when she called me to see if she could move in. I wondered how she could be running such a successful online business if this was the case, but it didn't seem to bother her.

"Thanks," I muttered as I walked to the freezer.

She could keep her pizza. I wanted every topping on mine after such an intense shift, and there was no way I would fudge a supreme while waiting on laundry and the sunrise. Instead, I heated up some water on the stove to make the last of the ravioli.

I made a mental note to buy more ravioli.

Jade returned, lugging her large laundry hamper behind her and quickly disappeared up the stairs. When she returned sans hamper, she pulled a spoon out of the drawer and stuck it into the bowl of the mixer.

When she pulled it out, she had a good clump of cookie dough on the spoon.

"Would you like to try some?"

"Raw cookie dough makes my stomach upset," I replied.

"Oh... all right. More for me." She shrugged and ate it off the spoon.

I wanted to leave so badly because this is not how I planned to spend my time... but with my laundry going, I was stuck.

Chapter Eight

Eight: Jade

I watched as Jesse sat, defeated, at the counter. It looked like he was ready to do something else, *anything else*, but had decided it would be much better to stay at the house until morning. When he had first walked in, I caught a whiff of smoke. As if he had sat at a bonfire for hours. I vaguely recalled him mentioning what he did for work, but now I couldn't recall it off the top of my head. That wouldn't do at all if I was going to be his roommate.

"Remind me what you do?" I looked up from the bowl of cookie dough as I spooned a good heap onto the cookie sheet.

Considering I had found the two I owned, and he had one, I had enough cookie sheets to make all of the dough without needing to wait for batches to rotate through the oven. However, now that I thought about it, I probably couldn't fit them all in the oven at once. These were too large to turn sideways, and I knew from experience that the cookies didn't bake as well if there were two large pans on the racks. So, it'd have to be one at a time tonight.

At least I could at least *prepare* all of the cookie sheets at once, I thought.

"I'm a firefighter," Jesse said curtly.

I remembered now. But his voice had a defeated tone. Maybe he just didn't want to talk to me. I felt a surge of anger flicker.

Calm down, I chided myself. *At least try to figure out why he sounds annoyed. It might not be about you.*

I'd seen firefighters a few times as a nurse. I remembered the burns a bad fire could give a firefighter, and it wasn't pretty. I'd never asked about their jobs at the hospitals I'd worked at, but the firefighters I had met who had come to visit their friends after a fire had been simply lovely. A little jaded perhaps, but who wouldn't be jaded after a career like that?

I'd met policemen who were the same way when coming to visit an officer who had been severely injured in the line of duty. It all depended on what kind of career people were in.

"That would explain why I smelled smoke then, when you came in," I said. "You've been doing the job a while?"

He nodded.

"And you've seen a few things?"

"Where are you going with this?" He now looked at me with exasperation. "Jade, I appreciate that you want to get to know me, but this is not the way to do it."

Okay now I was mad.

He had no right to tell me the "right way" to get to know someone. After all, he obviously wasn't the expert in the room in terms of friendliness.

I turned back to the oven and began spooning cookie dough with more ferocity than I intended. Jesse was really grating on my nerves. At the hospital, it looked like firefighters enjoyed working on a team and helping others – as doing so gave them the external stimuli to be happy. All the firefighters I'd seen come to the hospital to help their teammates had been exhausted, but seemed fulfilled with their lives. Jesse didn't seem to enjoy the teamwork, nor did he seem all that fulfilled in life when he returned.

He just seemed bitter and angry, and I was not about to let this man—a total stranger, really—boss me around when he wasn't even supposed to be home right now anyway.

I chucked the spoon into the sink and spun back to face him. He was just sitting scrolling on his phone, utterly oblivious to my fury. "I'm just trying to get to know you, Jesse. If we're going to be living together, even if it's meant to be something more akin to you just popping in for a night or two as if this was a hotel," I said, my voice clearly tense. "And I'm not looking for specifics on what you've seen if you're wondering. My time in the nursing industry has taught me never to ask for specifics from a few specific careers. Firefighting is one of them. I'm just trying to make basic conversation and you're frankly being rude. I *know* you probably don't want to talk about the details, but that's why I *didn't ask* about the details. I've seen the burns firefighters can get when their protective gear fails, and I'm not about to ask to see your scars. Geez, I'm just trying to be friendly; the least you could do is not be such a grump."

I trailed off.

I realized that I might have overstepped, but I glanced at Jesse's face to see how he took this. His eyes had narrowed. Even if he wasn't expecting to be entirely friendly with his tenant, a landlord was usually at least amicable with them. It helped to make sure that the tenant would be less likely to destroy things in a rage on the way out, I'd heard from my previous landlord.

But now that I looked at him again, Jesse didn't seem to care about the money it would take to fix things. He seemed the type to go after me in court if I *did* cause more than normal wear and tear that I didn't own up to and try to put right. There was just something to the stern countenance he wore currently that told me it would be better to keep to what I had learned from watching previous roommates lose their life savings than try to test him.

In that manner, anyway.

I was beginning to think I should apologize and then hide in my room.

"It is always sad when gear fails, even if it's not your own," Jesse finally said, taking me by surprise. "Some of the worst things I've smelled have come from failing gear."

I didn't need to ask for clarification. Burning flesh was a smell that I'd gotten the occasional whiff of as well as I walked past the emergency room. It wasn't pretty. Made me want to vomit every time. Thankfully, that was only in the beginning. I had learned to suppress the gag reflex enough to be able to treat those patients with the dignity they deserved.

The oven beeped at us, and I put the first sheet of cookies in before setting a timer.

"Why cookies?"

Jesse's voice caught me off-guard, but thankfully I was able to keep from hitting the wrong number on the timer.

"I felt like it." I shrugged. "Why? Do I need a reason to bake cookies?"

"Curiosity."

I nodded slowly. Single-word answers would get old real fast, but I was glad he was at least sharing anything with me.

"What got you into firefighting if I may ask?" I said. "And you don't have to give me the full story. If you don't want to, I mean."

The way he appeared to be entirely set on making sure I got as little information as possible was interesting, but I was determined to make the most of this conversation.

"I got into firefighting because I wanted to help people. I found that I had a passion for it. Now, I just want to be sure that the fires go out without any injuries. We're not always that lucky."

He looked at his lap, and I let the silence settle over the two of us as I continued spooning out cookie dough. It kept me half-occupied, so he was only getting the surface-level questions. I didn't want to be the reason he had issues sleeping tonight. Memories always needed to be locked away in this kind of work, and I didn't want to bring them up without meaning to.

I wasn't even sure what purpose bringing them up would have served, even if I *meant* to do that to him. It was one thing to do it without knowing what brought the memories up. It was another entirely to torment him by doing it on purpose and pushing until I found the right questions and issues to raise around him.

"So, what did you forget when you left for the shift at the fire station?" I ventured into some different territory as I finished rolling the last of the cookies out. "You said you forgot something when you arrived."

"I have a bag that I keep in my car. I must have brought it inside meaning to do laundry and never got around to it until tonight. Not that it's any of your business," he snapped.

"Geez. Calm down. I'm just making light conversation," I said, trying to keep the sarcasm out of my voice. "it's not like I'm asking to rifle through your drawers. I like to save that until at least our fourth conversation."

He didn't laugh.

I rolled my eyes. "Why is making conversation with you like pulling teeth? It's not like I'm trying to get your social security."

"Because it's a fluke that I'm even home tonight!" Jesse revealed as he stood up from his seat rather abruptly. "I only came home because

I forgot something, and I only forgot it because you've interrupted my normal schedule. Now, leave me be!"

He walked out of the kitchen. A few moments later, I heard the master bedroom door slamming shut.

I could feel my face, hot with anger and some form of embarrassment I couldn't quite name. I'd just been trying to be friendly. If he hadn't wanted to make conversation, he could've retreated to the master bedroom the moment he'd started his laundry. Why sit in the kitchen unless he wanted to talk?

I sighed heavily.

The oven timer dinged at me. As I pulled the first sheet of cookies out and put another batch in the oven to cook, I was beginning to feel like I had made a mistake renting from Jesse Delaney. The rent was fantastically priced, but there were drawbacks that had not been entirely apparent on the listing.

In the interest of fairness, I supposed that it wouldn't have been something he would have wanted to disclose, especially since he had been entirely upfront about not being home often.

I mean, how do you put "landlord is the absolute worst" on a rental listing?

When he'd said that he would be gone most of the time, I thought it meant that I would only see him for a few minutes each night and from there, we could make the conversations that would lead to an amicable acquaintanceship. I hadn't realized that he never, ever wanted to interact with me.

"It's not like I'm asking to be your girlfriend, you grump," I muttered. "Why are you like this?"

I had such an urge to ask him who in the world had hurt him so irrevocably, so deeply. Surely, he had been hurt by someone close to him at one point for him to be so grumpy. So mad at the world.

The desire to listen to my music at the loudest volume I could stand suddenly disappeared. Instead, I headed upstairs and grabbed my Bluetooth headphones. Funny little contraptions they were, since they used bone conduction technology to do their work instead of functioning like a normal pair of earbuds.

They worked wonders for hearing what was going on around me. They allowed me to watch a show while still listening for the timer. My laundry could wait until the cookies were all done in the oven—which would only take another twenty or thirty minutes since each batch took about fifteen minutes total to cook.

"If you want to be like that, then we don't have to be friends," I muttered as I turned my phone on again to listen to a show as I put dishes away. "But I'd like to be treated civilly. It's not like I'm breaking any rules by simply trying to make conversation."

If he tried to make the rule that conversation with him, unless it was about the rent and his duties as landlord, was off-limits, I was out of here. The only person I knew in town was Maria, and it was so disheartening to literally be living with someone who very clearly didn't want anything to do with me. I needed to be able to enjoy something about the place, and so far, his personality was not the winning aspect of the property. That was still by far and large the commute to the store that Maria and I had leased out.

Since Jesse was set on being such a whiner tonight, I started texting Maria to figure out when we wanted to open the store. We'd have to do some decorating, of course, and I had to put some jewelry up for display. We'd need a case or shelf for earrings since those were my best sellers.

I'd probably be spending the night beading. There was nothing wrong with that. I'd spent a good portion of the afternoon beading, too. If we were going to be at all successful, I needed to increase how much I was producing so that we had stuff we could sell at the store in addition to the commissions I took online.

And I'd have to update the description on my online shop. If people were in the area and wanted things now, they could come to the store instead.

Chapter Nine

Nine: Jesse

The next morning, I was out of the house before Jade even woke up. It was rather easy to do since I had already packed everything after getting her off my case about what I do and why I was home for the night. With my laundry already done, all I'd had to do was pack my little bag and put the rest of my laundry in my room – to be dealt with later after I returned home, but before my next shift.

On the drive to the ranch, I couldn't help but think of how the night before had gone. Jade had wanted to know some specifics about my job that I wasn't willing to share with *anyone* – whether or not they had seen the burns we could get from the fires we fought. The fact that she was a nurse before coming here should have taught her that there were just some careers that lent themselves to danger. Firefighting, police officers, military, and others all took specialized risks that others – such as jewelry makers – wouldn't understand.

I shook my head as I continued to drive along the highway. If she hadn't learned last night, I'd keep emphasizing that I liked my privacy. It was why I wasn't home all that often. The area I lived in had neighbors who liked to get together and get to know each other.

If she was all interested in making friends, she could make her stupid 'small talk' with them.

A couple of hours later, I arrived at the ranch. The dusty road reminded me of all the hours that I had spent keeping track of the cattle in my childhood, but nowadays, I preferred work with the horses.

My father waved to me from where he stood, glad to see that I had finally made it. I walked over to him, making sure to lock my truck on the way. It was less about not trusting anyone on the ranch and more about being sure everything would be safe. I had my good work boots in there. If those got stolen, I was going to have to find another pair in a hurry. And it wasn't easy to accomplish that.

"I wasn't sure you were coming after I didn't hear anything last night," my father said as I got closer. "What kept you from getting here?"

"I didn't get my laundry done in time, and I decided freshly cleaned laundry would make the drive easier," I admitted. Silently, I chided myself for forgetting to text my dad.

I didn't want to be the one to tell him that I had basically forgotten my bag and had then realized that laundry was important to do on the one day or so I was home each month. It was embarrassing. The less he knew about the situation, the better.

"And the renter situation?"

"She's all moved in, and it's been... well, it's been tough," I admitted. "She doesn't understand my need to get away from everything. Wanted to talk last night. Just... just talk."

"Well, what do you expect when you've moved someone new into the home?" My father gave me a look. "Jesse, I could have told you that no matter who you let move in to give you that rent, you would have been taking the risk that they wouldn't be able to understand that you're not that much of a talkative guy. Though, I might also say that talking to someone every now and again certainly wouldn't kill you. Sometimes your mom and I worry that you're getting too isolated, only talking to family or your work colleagues. Most people need friends too, you know."

I gave my father the largest frown I could muster.

"I swear, all four of you picked careers that jaded the lot of you," he said, shaking his head. "I can't understand why you would do that to yourselves, but if those are your passions, then I have no ground to stand on. Your mother and I were the ones who told you to be sure to find something to do that would fulfill your dreams."

"We just all like to *help*," I clarified. "What comes from years doing it comes from interacting with the stupidest of the people around us because, more often than not, they are the ones making the trouble that everyone needs to be rescued from."

My father shook his head. With that, I went to help groom the horses. I needed to be able to do something with my hands that wasn't holding a water hose spurting water out at such speed that I could feel the hose vibrating.

It wasn't but a couple of hours later that I heard my phone going off in my pocket. I soothed the horse I was working with before walking away to climb the ladder. It continued to ring, so I knew that it was not a text. I wondered who could be calling. Quietly, I prayed it wasn't Jade.

When I reached the top of the loft, I answered my phone, not taking time to see who was actually calling.

"Hello?"

"Jesse, finally!"

The voice of my superior at the fire station came through. This was odd. The only time he ever really called me was to see if I could fill in for someone before I left to go out of town for my days off. I wondered what he needed now because, as far as I was aware, everyone on the crew coming in after me was healthy right now. No one was ill. Not even a headache plagued that crew.

"What do you need, sir? Did I forget something at the station?"

"No, Jesse. We need everyone to come in for a meeting tomorrow morning. Don't worry; it's not about performance or anything. It is important though. I thought I'd give you a heads-up today so that you're not panicking about trying to make the drive back and arrive on time from wherever you go when you're not on duty here," my boss said.

I managed to hold back a groan.

"All right. I'll get back to town tonight then," I said. "I hope this is worth the drive I have to make. I wasn't planning to return until Saturday."

"Well, I'm not sure I can say anything more other than we need everyone there," he said. "Thanks for understanding."

With that, I hung up the phone. I held it tightly in my hands, wishing that I could just chuck it over the loft railing and watch it shatter. Unfortunately, that would make it difficult for Jade to get in touch with me if something were to go wrong, and it would mean I'd have to get a new phone.

I took a deep breath, put it back in my pocket, and climbed down the ladder before continuing with the work so rudely interrupted.

The rest of the day went by far too quickly. I spent most of the day working with the horses, which was truly my happiest place on the ranch. Working as a firefighter was my way of emulating what my elder brothers had shown to me and what Dad had once shown in his work. It was a way of giving back to the community around me, even though now it had started to wear on my soul.

At dinner that evening, I could hardly eat anything, as much as I appreciated that my father had gone through the trouble of making burgers.

"You're picking at your food, Jesse," Mom said as I took a bite slowly. "Is something wrong?"

"I have to leave after dinner," I said. "I got a call from my supervisor, but he didn't give many details. I'm just tired, and I'd rather stay here." I shrugged, "but duty calls."

My father raised an eyebrow. "You were just telling me this morning about how happy you were to be here. Do you really have to go tonight?"

"I need to be at the fire station tomorrow morning. Depends on how long the meeting is but I'll let you know if I need to stay in Lantana longer than that," I said. "I'm sorry, but I'll need to leave after dinner."

My parents exchanged a look. I don't think they were happy about it either. But we chatted a bit and finished our burgers, and I hugged my mom before re-packing my bag and heading out to the truck.

The drive back to Lantana didn't feel as though it took nearly as long as it took to return to the ranch, and I always wondered if it was because I wanted to get things over with in Lantana or if it was because Lantana was technically home despite still having a bedroom at the ranch.

Once I arrived home, my stomach started to growl. Again. It seemed I hadn't gotten enough food at the ranch, and I had completely forgotten that I had wanted to stop on the way home.

I heaved a sigh as I got out of the truck. Jade was going to have a *field day* with me, and I was going to have to endure it as I got dinner together. That's when I noticed that Jade's car wasn't in the driveway. I figured she must have gone out for the evening. If I left my truck in the driveway, she'd know that I was back, but she would also be less likely to block me in.

Also, then she'd be prepared to see me, and she might not try to start any stupid conversations again.

When I walked in, I smelled the herbs and bright scent of pesto. Someone had gotten their hands on a lot of fresh basil, or they had made pesto from a mix.

"Jesse? Is that you?"

Jade's voice came from the kitchen.

"I thought he wasn't home often."

This voice I was unfamiliar with.

My stomach sank. She had company over. Not only was Jade home but she had company. Maybe she had parked her car in the garage since she'd thought I was going to be away for a few days.

Great, I thought. *Just great.*

That was honestly the last thing I had expected to walk into, but I supposed it was also her home. She should feel like she can have company when she wants to. However, this was very much not wanted tonight.

First, I had to delay my arrival at the ranch for laundry. Now, I had to return home for a meeting tomorrow, and must also endure the threat of company when I just wanted food and sleep. And maybe a shower. Working on the ranch all day was hard work, and I knew I had been sweating up a storm.

I walked into the kitchen to find Jade at the stove with a young woman about her age, putting something in the fridge.

"Oh! You must be Mr. Delaney. I'm Maria Underwood. Jade has told me so much about you."

"It's nice to meet you," I said, managing to keep my voice polite. Somehow.

"She doesn't bite, Jesse," Jade said with a bit of a laugh. "But you told me you were going to be gone for a few days. Plans change? Again?"

I heard the challenge in her voice. I had promised her a house mostly to herself, and this was the second night in a row I was breaking that promise.

"I'm needed at the station tomorrow," I said plainly.

"Would you like some pasta? It's my mother's recipe," Maria said as if attempting to cut the tension between the two of us. "We have plenty to share. The recipe for the pesto makes far too much for just two of us, even if we split the leftovers."

I was about to refuse when my stomach growled.

"I suppose some pesto pasta would do me well," I said, resigned. "A small helping."

"With a stomach growling like that, I think it would be best for you to serve yourself," Jade said. "Good thing we hadn't started the noodles yet. I'll put more in, just to be safe. Whatever we don't eat tonight, we can put in the sauce and put in the fridge for tomorrow."

Maria nodded. I didn't care *what* they did.

"Save me a plate."

With that, I went to shower quickly. It would be better than staying in the kitchen while they talked. Though it would only buy me a little bit of time since my stomach was absolutely growling at me, I wondered what they were talking about that had been put on hold while I was in the room.

When I finished, and had gotten dressed in some sweats and a clean T-shirt, I returned to the kitchen. Jade had indeed kept a plate for me, with a generous helping of pasta and pesto on the plate. Instead of saying anything, I decided to take the plate into my room.

"Oh, please don't go," Maria said. "I'd love to hear all about what you do for work. It's got to be hard, working as both a firefighter and a ranch hand. How do you make the time for it all?"

I could tell there was genuine curiosity in her voice. This woman was no more malicious than the men at the fire station that I worked with, but I had no desire to answer her questions.

"Maria."

Jade's tone indicated that she had warned her friend of what to say and ask if I came home, and it seemed that Maria was not following the script. I had to appreciate this because Jade did appear to care... even if there was every reason in the world that she could have told Maria to pester me because I wasn't answering her own questions.

"What? It's not like I'm asking him how the job has impacted him mentally," Maria said. "I've seen the burns, too, Jade. You're not the only nurse here. I'm just genuinely curious to know how he's handling all the physical labor from working as a firefighter *and* a ranch hand. I don't think that I could do either, let alone do it all at once."

"It is rather physically challenging," I said, putting my plate in the microwave. The first bite was too cold for my taste. "It's not the easiest thing in the world, doing both jobs. But I manage. One keeps me fed. The other keeps my soul warm."

This is what I told people to keep them from asking how I was able to afford this house. Of course, with the money from both jobs, it was usually a no-brainer for people to assume that I had saved my money until I could buy it in cash. Things had, at one point, been that simple.

"I imagine the money's good if you're reliable," Jade mused.

"It must be if he's still doing both jobs," Maria continued.

My food finished in the microwave. For the sake of not appearing rude or flippant, I sat down at the counter. And mentally braced myself. It appeared that Maria was not going to heed whatever warning Jade had given her about my attitude.

"It is money enough in this economy," I said.

Chapter Ten

Ten: Jade

Money enough, he said, but the look on his face told me that he was sick of talking to us. To be honest, I hadn't even thought that he would entertain the conversation. To know that he was extending that courtesy to Maria warmed my heart a little, but it still hurt that he would hardly acknowledge me if I was here alone with him. What made Maria different?

"Have you told him yet, Jade?" Maria looked at me.

I shook my head. He had only just arrived home, and she had started asking the questions as soon as he showed any interest in staying to have a discussion with us.

"I'll handle *that* discussion, Maria," I replied. "Just... go easy. Please."

Jesse raised an eyebrow, looking between the two of us. He swallowed whatever was in his mouth. He opened his mouth to say something, but Maria cut him off.

"So, how long have you been a firefighter?"

"Long enough to have burn scars on my hands and long enough that I'm thinking I've had enough," Jesse finally said. He let his fork clatter to the plate and looked daggers at Maria.

"You could've just said 'five years' or whatever," Maria pointed out. She looked at me. "Does he talk to you like that too?"

I could tell I needed to step in before things escalated.

"Maria. Enough. Let him decompress. He's clearly had a schedule change, and he's clearly angry about something," I said as I put my plate in the sink.

"You're right about that, Jade."

His flippant nod punctuated the end of the statement.

"Well." Maria pursed her lips. "That's certainly an unimpressive attitude."

"Maybe I just want to be able to *relax* after getting home from such strenuous activities," Jesse half-yelled as he took the rest of what was on his plate into the master bedroom.

I sighed.

"And this is what you have to live with? I think I see why the rent was so cheap," Maria thought out loud as the door slam echoed in the kitchen. "If he knew he wasn't going to do well with someone else in the house, why rent out the top floor and let you treat the rest of the house like you own it, too?"

"I have no idea, Maria," I said softly. "But please. Just because that's what he's like tonight doesn't mean that's what he's like all the time."

Maria gave me a look; one I knew well from the many hours of classwork we had done together. She didn't buy it.

"Well, if that's the case, then I guess I just have bad timing," Maria eventually said. "But, Jade, I would seriously look into a high-yield savings account. Let that money sit, gather the interest, and get your own apartment or something. Because, *yikes*. Is he even safe to live with? I mean, this is not great behavior."

"I'll be all right, Maria. I promise," I said. "I think he's just used to being a bit of a hermit. Now, as far as the rest of what I wanted to tell him goes, I'll do my best to say it before we see him tomorrow, but I can't guarantee anything."

"Well, you're just trying to be nice. If it doesn't work, it doesn't work, and you've done all that you can about it." Maria shrugged.

I laughed a little.

"If you're done, then we can get started on these dishes, and then, it's time for a good night's rest."

With that, we rinsed off the dishes and put the leftover pasta and pesto in the fridge. We decided to just run the dishwasher in the morning, and Maria was almost happy to be leaving the house.

"Well, I'll be happier hanging out here again when he's not around," Maria admitted. "I'm not a big fan of your landlord there. He's... he's far too isolated for my tastes." She wagged a finger at me. "And he might be cute, but I'd steer clear if I were you."

"*Maria!*" I practically started giggling and half-shoved her out the door. "I can guarantee that is *not* something you have to worry about."

"Good."

With that, I waved to Maria as she walked out to her car. She waved goodbye to me before she drove away.

I walked back inside and then realized that it had gone absolutely silent in the house. Part of me had hoped that this would only be the case when he was away, but it appeared that he was content to continue whatever schedule he had been using before I came into the picture. It was rather isolating, but I was determined to break through that.

Instead of just taking it on the chin, I walked over to the master bedroom and knocked on the door.

"Jesse, she's left if you would like to eat at the table or something," I said. "I'm sorry. I did try to warn her that you don't like to be interrupted at dinner or answering questions."

There was no response. I couldn't even hear him shuffling towards the door to say something to me.

Instead of waiting for something to happen, I decided that I had done my part. If he didn't want to forgive me for doing my best to stop Maria, then that was his problem.

I walked back to the kitchen to start the dishwasher. I stopped when I heard the master bedroom door open.

Jesse walked in, put his plate in the dishwasher, and then walked back to his room.

"Wait!" I said, attempting to stop him from returning to his room. "I have something else I'd like to-"

The door slammed before I could finish speaking.

"To say..." I finished, letting the words hang in the air.

I let out a sigh. Then, I went to start the dishwasher. Fine. If he didn't want to hear what I was doing tomorrow, then he could learn when I showed up at the fire station. I had a feeling he had been asked to come to the same meeting I had been since it was all about the annual fundraiser for the local fire stations.

Perhaps working on the fundraiser together would allow us to see that the other wasn't so bad. Or, at least, allow me to give him a better chance to get to know me.

After starting the dishwasher, I went up to my room. A glance at the clock revealed that it was only seven p.m. I didn't know exactly what time Jesse went to bed when he had meetings at ten in the morning, but I imagined that he would still go to bed as if he were getting up at four-thirty.

It was entirely too early for me.

However, I respected that he had a routine. I connected my Bluetooth headphones to my desktop and decided I was going to finish this pair of earrings before the meeting tomorrow.

They were almost done. I just had one more line of beads to finish on one of the earrings and to add the posts to the felt backs.

These were smaller, and would cost less to sell. They were also easier to whip up for fundraising. I would, of course, create some that dangled because those always sold well, but there was a reason I was doing more than just the stand. These designs took time to bring to life. With being asked so late in the game, I had already put my intentions on my site. Prices hadn't raised any to cover this, but I was glad to see the sales rolling in and people noting in their orders that they had actually ordered more than they had originally meant to because of the cause I was raising money for.

Being honest usually helped in these situations.

As I watched my show – a typical sitcom where the lead was always frustrated in love – I strung the last of the beads onto the thread I was using.

Once they were all on, I tied it all off in a knot on the back and found some good-sized posts that would hold these up. It was less of a post and more of a hoop earring clasp, but it worked. People ordering from me knew that I didn't do small beading. These were always the smallest that one could order, and I didn't keep much of them in stock because I found them too easy to make.

The logic said I should be making them far more often, but I liked the challenge of the bracelets, necklaces, and the heavier earrings. Besides, they often didn't have complicated patterns because I kept all my jewelry simple. It was all supposed to be something that could be worn every day.

A couple of hours later, I shut off my computer and the lights. It was bedtime. I had to be up early tomorrow, and I didn't want to get to the meeting late.

The next morning, I woke up and found Jesse still home. He was in the kitchen, making some waffles with a waffle maker that I had somehow missed when I moved in.

"Those smell delicious. Have enough batter for two there?" I looked over curiously, rubbing the sleep out of my eyes.

He glanced over at me.

"I didn't realize you were still asleep..." He pursed his lips. "Yeah. I should have enough for two."

He then passed me a plate with a couple of fresh waffles on it. I smiled softly before taking it to the counter. I found the butter and syrup and then started to eat. Jesse said nothing as I ate and he manned the waffle iron.

Part of me wanted to say something, but I supposed it was not that hard to learn when we got to the fire station.

"What time is your meeting?" I tried to make conversation.

"Ten this morning. Why do you ask?"

"I have somewhere to be around ten this morning as well," I admitted. "Jesse..."

"Well, that can be easily done, because once I leave, you're going to be able to leave. I'm going to go out early this morning and get some other things done," he said without giving me a chance to say anything more. "I'll see you when I see you next."

"Oh. All right."

I didn't know what to say now. However, I soon learned it did not matter. Jesse simply unplugged the waffle iron, scooped two of the waffles up from the plate of waffles, and walked to the front door. The front door opened, and then shut quickly. Outside, I could hear the crunching of the gravel under his shoes.

"Well, I suppose that leaves me time and space to prepare the display here before I take it out to my car." I sighed.

I finished my waffles and cleaned up the kitchen a little. The waffle iron was still hot, so really, all I did was put the dishes in the sink and let the waffle iron cool while I set up my display.

Upstairs, I pulled out the large posterboard that Maria and I had decorated. It looked a little bit like a school project, but that was all our budget would afford right now. It'd have to do. Hopefully, the fire fighters we were working with would understand that we were a new business and didn't have the same kind of budget that other businesses in the area had.

The poster board made the trip out to the car first. It was the largest thing I was taking. Therefore, it needed to be the first thing out to the car to make sure I had enough room for it. It managed to fit in the backseat without needing to be folded. If it had needed to be folded, I would have stuck it in the trunk. It did have a place to fold it that wouldn't be obvious, but I didn't want to have to do that.

Not if I could avoid it, anyway.

Once that was in the trunk, I gathered the jewelry that I was taking. It had mostly already been pulled aside from the reserves I kept for online orders, but I double-checked against the list I had on my phone.

The simple earrings, bracelets in red, necklaces with orange and yellow in the beads... it was all here. I packed a few of my displays to be safe since I wasn't sure what kind of an area we'd have to display what we were selling.

I also had to wonder what Maria was bringing. She had promised that it would be just as spectacular as my jewelry but hadn't given me any indication of what it would be.

I shook my head.

"I can learn that when I get there. I should probably leave a little early so that I can set up before the rest of the firefighters arrive..."

I glanced at my phone's clock. It was only eight-thirty in the morning. I could probably wait another half an hour before I left. If the GPS on my phone was right, it'd take about a half hour to get there this early with traffic, and I wanted about a half hour to set everything up. It was mainly the jewelry displays I suspected would give us trouble.

I was just about to head back upstairs to start beading something else when my phone buzzed at me.

It was just a text from Maria. I walked inside anyway and checked it. There were just some days that I couldn't see the screen on my phone outside for the life of me. Today was one of those days.

Need help setting up. Come to fire station early, please.

Maria... I sighed. What had she brought that would require two people? Had she actually taken a set of curtains to show off? Unless they were red and orange and yellow – like a fire – I doubted that it would be something that people would be interested in today.

Regardless, I texted her back that I'd be there as soon as possible and got in my car.

The drive to the fire station was indeed about a half hour, and there I found Maria struggling to set up not curtains, but a table to put her purses and a few pictures of her curtains on. At least she had done something sensible.

"Maria, where did you get this table?" I asked as I walked over. "And why is it giving you so much trouble?"

"I bought it second-hand so that I could have something for the store to set my purses on," she admitted. "Help, please."

Chapter Eleven

Eleven: Jesse

Upon arriving at the fire station, I noticed a ton of cars in the parking spots. Way more than usual. I frowned a little as I pulled into a spot. What was going on? I knew we were having a meeting with all the firefighters who worked out of this station, but this appeared to be far more than that in the parking lot. We had enough parking spaces to keep everyone happy if everyone needed to come in. There were cars parked on the street in the parallel parking spots today, which almost never happened. Not unless some large event was going on nearby, and we usually knew of those ahead of time.

The only other excuse I could think of for all of the hustle and bustle was that it was fundraising season. My stomach dropped at the thought.

If it was indeed fundraising season, I had lost track of all the time. I usually took vacation this time of year and left to go to the ranch for a few weeks because I wanted nothing to do with the fundraising. However, I'd needed my days for other things this year because the ranch had had a tough run last winter.

I walked inside to find a bunch of artisans setting up their little stands. A glance at my watch revealed that I was about five minutes early for the meeting, so that was fine. What was *not* so fine was that I recognized someone.

I saw Jade and Maria setting up a small table with purses, earrings, bracelets, and other useless items.

How long had they known they were going to be doing this?

Instead of immediately going to talk to them, I decided the best thing to do would be to put some distance between us, especially after our disagreement last night. Also, I didn't want the rest of the men to realize that this was the woman I had allowed to move in with me. If they knew her name and face, I would never hear the end of it. And that was absolutely not what I wanted to happen.

Eventually, the fire chief got everyone settled down. There had been some excited chatter. I imagined that had been because the others recognized some of the vendors from years previous. Since I always took vacation, this was the first year I would be around to help with the fundraiser – which I thought would be an utter disaster. Fundraising has never been my area of expertise, and I figured my helping out would really raise the risk of totally bungling the event.

Fundraising is all about making people feel like they're a part of something. Those types of superficial connections are really not my strength.

"Thank you all for coming, especially those of you who were not scheduled to work today," the fire chief said. "Now, we have a few changes to the roster this year. Some of the businesses we've worked with in the past have decided that they're too busy this year, but it's all right. We have a brand-new business here in town to help us out, and I'd like everyone to give a round of applause to these two lovely young women for offering their help last minute so that we have a full roster of shops for people to support us through."

The chief motioned towards Maria and Jade. They both looked a little embarrassed to be called out like that, but they smiled and waved to the crowd of firefighters.

I offered meager applause to keep up the appearance that I had no interest in this fundraising but to also show that I appreciated what they were doing. I may not have wanted to be a part of the fundraising, but I knew exactly how invaluable this season was for us.

There was a lag in the applause, and when the fire chief didn't step in, it became obvious he was waiting for the women to say something in the way of introduction.

"Thank you for inviting us to help," Jade said with a wide smile. "I know that it can be difficult to reach out to new members of the community, but we've got a good track record already. I sell my jewelry online as well, and opening a store was just the next step. In addition to the proceeds that are to be given to all of you at the end of your day of fundraising, I've already started collecting twenty percent of my proceeds in general from online sales to come to you guys at the end of the fundraising."

"Now, that's mighty generous of you," the fire chief said. Then, he turned to the crew of firefighters. "You all know the drill. Talk to the vendors, and find the ones you like. I will need at least one firefighter assigned to each stall on the day of the fundraiser, and we'll have plenty of posters to start going up tomorrow. Now, get going."

With that, we were left to our own devices. I immediately headed for the small table of refreshments to get some water. What were they going to do here? Had they accepted because they wanted to get their business started, or were they purposefully tormenting me because they knew how much I wasn't interested in building a connection with Jade.

Reasonably, they probably were just here because they wanted to help with the fundraiser. But I was worried. I knew my buddies would have a field day when they found out Jade was my new tenant. Objectively, she was very attractive, and I knew that's all my friends would see. A single, attractive woman living in my house.

After calming my stomach down a little bit with some water and some of the crackers, I walked over to Jade.

"Jesse! I swear I was going to tell you last night," Jade said when she saw me. "I just didn't have a chance to with everything going on. And this morning, you didn't give me much of a chance at all to say anything."

I studied the way she spoke, but I didn't really care.

"Next time you want to help fundraise, pick another department," I said coldly. "We get enough help from the businesses around here as it is, and I don't need my crew teasing me about living with a woman any more than they already do."

With that, I walked away to hide in a corner until the event was over. If I was careful, I'd be able to avoid the duties of having to sit at one of the stalls all day long in the heat. Then again, there would have to be a crew in the fire station in case a fire did break out. Maybe I could talk to the chief and be part of that crew.

It'd be a lot better for me than sitting around helping my roommate at her stall, or even suggesting that we know each other to the rest of Lantana.

I watched as Jade flittered off to talk to someone else after taking in the fact that I just didn't want anything to do with her. I was not okay mixing work and my personal life, and if that made her mad, then so be it. She'd only been renting from me for a few days, and she was already climbing all over my business.

One of the other firemen came over to me.

"That Jade is a pretty one," he said. "It's no wonder you haven't told us much about her. Knew you'd have some competition," he winked and nudged me in the ribs.

"No—" I began, but he cut me off.

"She'll do great in the dating scene here in Lantana if she's not already dating someone else. Do you have any news to share with us?"

"Shut it, Lance," I said through gritted teeth. "I do not have any interest in her. She's just a roommate."

"Just a roommate?" Lance raised his eyebrows. "Why do you sound so angry when you say it? You know, I've been watching, and you've barely spoken two words to the lady. I thought that a *roommate* would at least get the privilege of seeing the same civil Jesse Delaney we see on shift. You may not like her, but that doesn't mean that you get to ignore her like this, Jesse. It's not right."

I turned to look Lance in the face. As much as I knew he was right, I also wanted to wipe the smug little smirk off his face.

"What of it? I'm not into her. I don't need to talk to her. You talk to her if you think someone should talk to her."

"Whoa. Chill," Lance said, the smirk leaving his face.

It was replaced with a deep frown.

"I don't like fundraising season," I said simply. "That's all." I was vaguely aware that I sounded unreasonable, and I searched for the words to make Lance understand. "I hate all the prep that goes into it. Why do you think I'm either on vacation this time of year or in the firehouse that day? It's not my jam. And I don't like that I'm going to have to put up with the prep in my own home now."

"Oh..." Lance pursed his lips. "Well, you could always *talk* to her, you know. That's usually the best way to work through these kinds of things. She can't read your mind, so she's never going to know that's why you're mad unless you actually tell her."

"What, have you been going to therapy all of a sudden?" I raised an eyebrow.

This was very out of character for Lance. While therapy was the norm for firefighters who had been working in the field for a certain number of years, I only checked in with a therapist once a year. I found that working on the ranch helped me remember that there were always better things out there than the carnage that could come from a fire. Even my therapist had said that as long as I didn't start showing signs of anxiety or depression, a check-in once a year and the ranch would be a perfect way to combat the stress of firefighting.

"Yeah," Lance admitted. "It's hard to remember the tricks she teaches me, but I at least remember that one. Part of my anger issues. I need to remember to vocalize before I explode, or the explosion's only going to be much worse."

I nodded slowly.

"I just don't like to talk about my personal life at work. It makes me uncomfortable when they mix together," I said simply.

Lance nodded slowly.

With that, Lance left me alone and walked off to talk to another of the vendors. I remained in my little corner, sipping water and making small talk with the firefighters who came to talk to me. At least most of the firefighters were more concerned with how I was feeling than with why I was in the corner. Most even bought the idea that I was struggling with feeling a little under the weather and didn't want to get the vendors sick. A few did suggest I talk to the chief to find someone to work with for the fundraising, but I simply nodded. I didn't want to deal with that today.

I'd talk to him next time I was on duty to see if I could be part of the firefighting crew that day instead of working one of the stalls with a vendor. I didn't need to be part of the fundraising aside from helping set up the posters. I hoped.

I glanced in the direction of where Jade and Maria had set up. They were now talking to the fire chief, but neither seemed to notice that I was playing quiet in the corner. I hoped they wouldn't.

Until George, one of the men from my crew, walked over to me.

"I thought I saw you!" George smiled at me softly. "The chief wants to see you. He's over there talking to Jade Santana – the bead lady."

"Bead lady, huh?" I raised an eyebrow. "And why has she gained that title?"

Of course, I already knew. Jade obviously worked with beads—which was therefore why she was so mad I'd tried to be helpful by putting her 'beading table' in the pantry. But I didn't want to let on that I knew Jade on a personal level.

"Have you seen what she makes with beads? She's got *talent*," George said. "Anyway, chief wants to see you. Don't know why. Didn't ask. I think it may have something to do with the fact that this is the first year you're here for the fundraising and not on vacation."

I nodded slowly as a pit opened in my stomach. Of course, that would be why he wanted to talk to me. But why around Jade's set-up?

I walked over, very much *not* excited to see what it was all about.

Chapter Twelve

Twelve: Jade

I shifted my weight nervously between my feet as we waited for Jesse to come over. Why the fire chief felt that it would be a good idea to have Jesse help us out, I didn't know. If any firefighter was going to help us out, I'd rather it be someone who was excited to see what we were selling, and not my landlord. Especially since that landlord had already decided to hate me.

Eventually, Jesse joined us.

"Ah, good." The fire chief smiled. "Jesse, as our most senior firefighter here, you're not on the advertising crew."

"May I ask what I will be doing, then?" Jesse's voice came out icy.

I didn't blame him. This wasn't exactly how I had expected all of this to come out, either, but here it was.

"You'll be helping our newest volunteers figure out their booth," the fire chief continued. "I realize that you usually go on vacation this time of year, and I don't entirely blame you. Fundraising is difficult business. *However,* since you haven't taken it this year, I think this is where you'll be most helpful. Miss Santana here has already said that you know her, and I think that'll make the work easier."

"If I could protest, Chief—"

"Oh, don't worry about it," the fire chief continued, obviously not understanding the source of Jesse's hesitation. "These ladies are lovely, and I'm sure everything will go smoothly. Especially with the most senior of my firefighters. Right, Jesse? Nothing you can't handle."

Jesse's face looked pinched. "Yes, Chief."

"Thank you, Chief," I said softly, not sure how to diffuse the tension. "I think we can take it from here."

With that, the fire chief left us alone to start looking into how the other volunteers were getting along with the staff at the firehouse.

"Well, it's good to see you again, Mr. Delaney," Maria said. "I wasn't sure if Jade would get a chance to tell you about this before we got here. It seems that she did not."

Maria gave me a look that could have killed. I gulped hard. She was right. I had promised her that I would talk to Jesse. However, I had underestimated how much he hated to have normal conversations with someone like me. It seemed like no matter what I did, he was not going to believe that I had done this because it was a good thing to do instead of doing it to make him uncomfortable.

I cleared my throat.

"Well, we're here now," I said. "I don't think there's any use thinking about what we could have done differently or what we should do differently for next time. We're here. Let's get going on figuring out how to rearrange this table. Maria, I think you managed to buy the most unbalanced second-hand table in the world."

It had already collapsed once under the weight of the purses and the jewelry. I hoped that we wouldn't have to provide our own table for the booth, but if we did, this wasn't it. It'd have to do for the store; perhaps we could put snacks or something on it instead of the purses as Maria had originally been thinking.

Jesse heaved a sigh and helped us take the purses off the table. Then, he got down under the table and looked at all of the mechanics.

"You don't have it secured." He popped his head up from under the table. "It's supposed to click into place when it's secured. Like... so..."

He moved the bars holding the table up just a little more to each side. There was a loud, distinct *click* in the air.

"Let's see if that'll hold everything," I said.

Maria nodded. She set it up as it had originally been set up, and we waited with bated breath. When Jesse bumped into it getting up off the floor, it only wiggled. Nothing fell over, bar one of the stands of earrings that I had set up. It wasn't the best earring stand, but it was good enough for this meeting.

"Well. That would explain a lot," Maria said. "Thanks, Mr. Delaney. I didn't realize it was supposed to lock in place, but that would explain why it was so wobbly. I just didn't go far enough to hear the click."

"Indeed."

With that, Jesse turned to look at me.

"Could I see you to the side a moment, please, Jade?" He kept his tone as even as possible, though I could tell that he was not happy about anything that was going on.

I nodded.

"Maria, make sure nothing happens to the jewelry while we talk," I said.

With that, we walked off to the side. Jesse led me into one of the furthest corners of the fire station, perhaps to ensure that we would not be disturbed. Whatever the case, I was not excited. This corner had some light, but it appeared to be one of the worst areas of the fire station. Perhaps one of the oldest and most in need of repair.

"How long have you known about this? Honestly?" He looked at me expectantly.

"We were approached while setting up our shop yesterday," I said. "Honestly. I meant to tell you last night or this morning, but I had no chance to say anything because you took off almost as soon as you were finished with breakfast, and you slammed the door when I tried to talk about it last night. We both know how last night went with Maria, and I'm sorry about that. She's just naturally curious, despite my best efforts to keep her contained."

I had started looking at the floor for some reason, but now, I looked up to meet his eyes.

Jesse stared at me as if he was searching my face for any semblance of a lie or of unfaithfulness to the story. I let him. If this is what it took for him to believe that I honestly didn't mean to let this all blow up in his face this morning, then that's what it took.

"I just want to help you get the funds you're trying to raise. Honest," I added. "I've always wanted to do something like this, but with an online-only store, it's hard for people to believe that you're actually going to donate the money. With the announcement that I have a store location in Lantana, it makes a lot more sense that I'm coordinating with someone to do this."

He pursed his lips.

"Fine."

He shook his head.

"But know this, Jade," he continued, now looking me directly in the eyes with an intense gaze, "Know that this is my home. If you do anything that will hurt the reputation of the men who work here or myself, then I will never forgive you. This is what I have poured my life into. I expect you to respect it. This isn't some... fantasy."

I quelled the surge of anger that rose within me. No matter what I did, he still seemed determined to believe the worst in me. For no reason. "Jesse, I've seen the worst kinds of burns a firefighter can get on the job in my time as a nurse," I gently reminded him. "I understand how difficult it can be. All I want to do is help make sure you guys have enough money to do your jobs and stay safe. Is that going to be okay with you?"

He considered and then nodded curtly.

"What do you need me to help you with? Other than making sure that table isn't going to collapse while you're at the booth," he said.

"Well... that's a good question. I'm not entirely sure what we're supposed to do to set it up," I admitted. "Will the fire station be providing tables and chairs for us to use during the fundraising event? Will there be internet where we'll be sitting?"

He took me over to a large map and pointed to an outdoor expo center.

"This is where we'll be. There may be internet for the booths closer to the expo center's indoor auditorium, but a hot spot would be preferred so that we're not overloading the internet provider there," he said. "You'll have to provide your table and chairs, and I believe a canopy if you'd like cover from the sun."

I nodded slowly.

We could provide the tables and chairs. The canopy, I was less sure about. I knew renting one could get expensive. At the very least, I made a mental note to bring sunscreen.

Out loud, I added to my list: "And we'll need a portable credit card reader."

Jesse raised an eyebrow.

"How many people do you know who still carry cash on them everywhere they go?" I looked at him with a soft smile. "It'll be a lot better for fundraising if we have a portable card reader for people who want to purchase something there at the table. If they'd like to browse the rest of my collection, I'll also have business cards with the site on them."

"Fine, fine, fine," he grumbled. "Now, we can't exactly go to the expo center yet, but I'm supposed to help you make sure you have everything ready to go."

"Why don't we head to the store, then? Most of what we'll end up using is going to be there," I suggested. "We could take my car home, and then carpool to the store and back home. I think that'd be far more efficient than taking both cars to the store unless you had something else you wanted to do?"

He shook his head.

"It can wait. This is my job right now, and I guess I have to see it through. *Regrettably*," he said sarcastically. "Find your friend and let her know the plan. I'm going to head back to the house. I guess I'll see you there." He didn't sound happy about it.

With that, Jesse walked away from me and out towards his car. I saw him pause momentarily to talk to the fire chief, but I couldn't hear what they were talking about. Nor did I think I wanted to. Instead, I simply returned to where we had set up camp.

"Hey, Maria, I think it's time to take our little setup down," I said. "Jesse thinks it'd be a better use of our time to be sure that we have everything we'll need for the day of the fundraising. We'll be at the expo center's field, so we're going to need a canopy."

"I might be able to make something work. I have a large tarp at home, and we could drape my beaded curtains on the tarp," Maria said as she started taking the purses off the table. "Where's Mr. Delaney gone now?"

"So, we're going to drop my car off at home since it's on the way, and then he'll drive me to the store so that we can go over what we have and what we need," I replied. "I'll meet you there."

"All right. Hey, bring all the jewelry you've got set up here. I think I've got another idea for how we could set it up, and we've got better equipment for that at the store, anyway."

I nodded.

With that, I carried my jewelry out to the car. Jesse's truck was long gone. I had a feeling he had suggested we go now so he could leave. I think he needed some time to decompress from hearing that he would be working with me for the fundraising.

I shook my head. The last thing I needed to do to myself was make up theories.

I finished packing the car, and once Maria was all packed up, headed home.

Chapter Thirteen

Thirteen: Jesse

On my way home from the fire station, I gripped the steering wheel tightly. This insanity was why I always took vacation around this time of year. It was never easy. Putting up flyers was probably easier than having to work with someone as insistent as Jade. I'd had trouble getting her to understand that I didn't want to talk at home. This was just going to make it worse: I *couldn't* escape some of these conversations now. And I had a feeling she would at least use that to her advantage once or twice before the fundraiser happened.

However, the main reason I wanted to get home first was because I wanted to call my father and let him know that I wasn't going to be able to come up to the ranch at all for a few weeks. Things were too busy here now.

I quietly cursed for not having kept a better eye on the calendar for the fundraising meeting. Usually, they wouldn't call in someone who was on vacation and would put them on flyer and water duty for the days leading up to and the day of, respectively. Or would put them in the firehouse because it was easier than disrupting a schedule that was already set.

At least being in the fire station to handle any fires that came in was something that I could *handle*. This, not so much.

Upon arriving home, I sighed and got out of my truck. It was somewhat silly to get out, but I knew that I had some time before Jade arrived. At least ten minutes, I'd think. So, I was going to have this conversation in the fresh air. With that in mind, I dialed my father's number. The phone rang a few times, but I half-expected it to go to voicemail. This time of day, a call to him either went right to voicemail or I sat waiting for him to pick up.

My father picked up.

"Jesse. I didn't think I'd be hearing from you today. What's the verdict? The meeting?" he asked. "What happened?"

I let out a breath.

"It's fundraising season. Usually, I take a vacation and go to the ranch for a while, but I forgot to book my vacation this year. I've been put in charge of helping one of the businesses here put together their booth and making sure they have everything they need," I said. "I'm probably not coming until after the fundraiser itself, which is in a couple of weeks... if I'm remembering my dates right."

"I see. Well, we'll miss you," he said. "Have fun and stay safe. And Jesse? If it's not too much trouble, remember to smile. You and your brothers all got so jaded... and I hate to see it. At least your brothers did eventually find something to smile about again outside their jobs."

"And the ranch," I mentioned. "The ranch is my sanctuary, Dad."

"Of course."

With that, and some extra pleasantries, we hung up. And just in time, too. I heard a car pulling up into the driveway. When I turned to look, I found that Jade had just arrived home.

She got out of her car, holding her purse, and then dug in the backseat for something. I pretended not to watch as I got up into the truck, but I couldn't help but notice that she was quite slender for someone who didn't work a physically demanding job. I wondered what she did to keep her figure... but quickly shook those thoughts away.

That wasn't something I needed to worry about. Nor was it something I needed to ask her about. I was all right with her calling me a grump; that much might actually have some truth to it. However, I refused to allow her to find a reason to call me a creep.

"You ready or what?" I called to her, mainly to distract myself. "We don't have all day."

"Just a moment. The jewelry spilled while I was driving."

I held back a groan. It was just jewelry. Did it really matter if it was all neatly put together in the box just to take it inside?

When she was done, I noticed that she wasn't taking it inside or even setting it back in the backseat to be taken in when we returned. Instead, she got up into the truck with a small box that clearly locked.

"I forgot to lock it before I drove off," she said. "Now, to the shop. I'll give you directions, but Maria thinks we've got something better at the shop that I could use to display the jewelry for the fundraiser. But I'm not sure that she's on the same page I am."

I nodded slowly. Whatever it took to get this nightmare over with.

I drove in silence. Jade more or less followed suit, only breaking the silence to give me directions to the store. As I got closer, I realized I recognized the area. This area was known for having some more interesting, exotic local businesses around. One of my favorite Indian restaurants was around the corner from her store. Considering this area of town was mostly filled with immigrant-owned businesses, rent in this area typically stayed a bit cheaper which made it more accessible to families new to the USA, working to make a living as new citizens. Alternatively, I supposed, that also made it a great spot to start a business from scratch. Basically, I wasn't entirely surprised she had managed to snag a good rent on the property.

"Here we are," she said as we pulled into the parking lot. "We're still waiting on our sign to come in so we can put it up on the front entrance, but it's a sweet little store."

"I swear there was something here last year..." I said as I got out of the car. "Don't remember what it was. Wasn't all that interesting to me. Something too *niche*."

"From what we heard, it didn't get a lot of business," Jade said as we walked towards the store.

The only other car in the lot must have belonged to Maria, I realized. The lights in the store were on, and the only person who could have gotten in, who wasn't Jade, was her friend. While other people might have noted that Maria had arrived out loud, I kept all of this to myself. The sooner we finished here, the better. I just wanted to go home, open a bottle of wine, and quietly sip the evening away while watching a movie. By myself.

I didn't think that'd happen without Jade attempting to converse with me unless she went upstairs to do whatever it was she needed to do for her business. Maybe make more jewelry.

"So, what did we come here for? You said you had supplies here?," I asked.

"This!" Maria pulled something from the back room. "This is what I was thinking of Jade. With the beaded curtains in another color coming down to give a little bit of shade in the front, I think this would work to give us some shade."

She came out with a large, blue tarp. Probably some kind of a painter's tarp. I'd heard of worse being used to make a canopy for this fundraising event, but this wasn't going to work at all. They'd stand out for miles. And not in a good way.

"It might be cheaper, and easier, to just get some cheap fabric and seam it up nice," Jade said. "I think this is going to be too heavy for any of our poles to handle. If we're supposed to be supplying everything, we have a canopy frame for something akin to a tent at a wedding, not a tarp for camping, Maria."

"Yeah... I'm just worried about the cost," she said.

"Besides, if you use the fabric, you can reuse the cheap curtains if you decide you want to do an expo or something and it's outside. Save the tarp for a rainy day, literally," I offered.

"Someone knows what he's talking about," Maria said with a smile. "I think that's a better idea. So, we'll need probably some chiffon or some cotton."

"Linen, Maria," Jade said. "I think linen curtains would be perfect for the weather we're going to have. Maybe with a layer of cotton or two over them and the beaded curtains in another color to contrast. We want to get people interested, right?"

"That would look amazing!" Maria exclaimed, clapping her hands in growing excitement.

"Interest is a good thing at these things," I pitched. "However, I don't know how much success you'll find trying to sell this absolutely gaudy jewelry in person. The pictures are so much better online."

Maria audibly gasped as if I'd stabbed a cat.

Jade whipped around on her heels.

"Seriously? Are you even capable of having a single decent conversation where you don't say something completely unkind?" When I didn't answer, she continued. "Excuse you. No one asked for your opinion."

She began to stomp away, but then she spun around and pointed to me.

"I don't owe you an explanation for anything—not why I'm at the fundraiser, why I moved to Lantana, anything. But I tell you because I thought 'hey, maybe he'll be less of a jerk if he knows a bit about me.' Well, I'll have you know that my grandmother taught me how to make beaded earrings and jewelry when I was young, and now that she's passed on, this is how I keep her and my family's culture close. The fact that it earns me money as well is just a bonus," Jade said, though her voice cracked a little. "Do you even know what it feels like to lose someone that close to you, someone who taught you everything you know how to do? How dare you say that."

Maria put an arm around Jade's shoulders, glaring at me.

For once, I found myself speechless, and not because I didn't want to have a conversation. I hadn't realized she had had such a connection to someone through jewelry-making.

And honestly, I guess I had been pretty rude. But I didn't know how to answer Jade, so I stayed silent.

My great-grandfather had started the ranch, and I could only imagine how I would have reacted had she said anything with similar tactlessness to me about the ranch and the time I spent there. It would not have ended well.

"Why don't you go to the back room to calm down, Jade?" Maria finally said after realizing that there was nothing coming out of my mouth. "I want to talk to Mr. Delaney."

Jade nodded, walking away from the two of us into the back room. Then, Maria turned to me.

"I cannot believe you just said that to her," Maria said. "Jewelry's not for everyone. She knows this. But all the people who have called it gaudy before have been haters of immigrants on social media, and not someone she was living with. Either get it together and apologize to her or get out of her life. She doesn't need this hatred in her life. She's dealt with enough of it already."

With that, Maria followed Jade into the backroom.

I took a moment to look around the little store. If they were planning on making a booth, they had plenty of product to take with them. There were little display racks of necklaces, bracelets, and more stands of earrings on the tables than I could count. Maria had managed to find a way to hang her purses up without having to worry about hiding any of them behind another.

There were even beaded curtains behind things, with tags. It was all carefully curated to appear as pleasing as possible.

I didn't know what to do, so I sat on a stool in a corner and waited. I was Jade's ride home, and I was supposed to be answering questions about the fundraiser. I figured I'd wait a while, and if they didn't come out, then I'd just go home and let Jade get a ride with Maria.

Eventually, the two emerged from the back office.

"You're still here?" Maria noted, dryly.

"Yep."

Jade looked at me.

"I'm sorry I yelled," she said.

I wanted to apologize, but how do you apologize for insulting someone like that? I didn't know what to say, and the words seemed stuck in my throat, so I didn't say anything. The two women stared at me, and then Jade eventually forced the conversation to move forwards.

"Now, that table we used at the fire station, I think it's good but maybe a touch too small for a booth for a fundraiser – if we want to have two or three tables of products."

I nodded slowly.

Keeping my mouth shut was probably my best bet now, so that is exactly what I did. Whatever Jade thought of me now, I did not blame her because that was a heck of a thing to find out.

Chapter Fourteen

Fourteen: Jade

I attempted to keep a conversation going because I knew that Jesse tended to literally walk away from conversations. But something in my gut told me that I had blown it today. I pursed my lips. This was not good. He had gone silent, and Maria appeared to be upset with him – more so than I was, in fact.

Though his comment about my jewelry being 'gaudy' had cut me to the core, it appeared he had learned his lesson upon hearing that my grandmother had taught me how to make this kind of jewelry. Sure, it would be nice if he apologized, but even seeing him look chastised was a pretty big step.

"How many tables of products are we allowed to have at this fundraiser, Jesse?" I turned to him.

Perhaps keeping the conversation focused on why we were all here together would keep him engaged enough to stay until we were done.

"I don't know," he replied. "I usually take vacation. I'm gone. I don't attend this thing, and this will be the only time I do, most likely."

He didn't have to rub in the fact that he could take vacation when he wanted to if he planned it out right. I simply took a deep breath.

There was no reason to get mad with him when he was clearly on edge from the earlier outburst.

"Then, I'll have to ask someone else who's attended before," I said. "Maria, I think we need to make a running list of questions that Jesse's unable to answer so that we can take them to the chief or whoever is in charge of making sure this runs properly."

I saw a frown flicker across Jesse's face. He was probably thinking about how the chief had specifically entrusted our table to him because he thought Jesse would do such a good job. In truth, Jesse was not particularly useful because he had absolutely no experience with the event, and it looked like he was beginning to realize that.

"Didn't the chief give us a small packet?" Maria popped her head up from where she was behind the cash register stand. "I think it had a whole bunch of answers to those kinds of questions. Where did we put it?"

"Probably the filing cabinet in the office. I'll get it."

I took a deep breath and headed to the back of the store. There were not a lot of places these documents could hide, and I knew that we had stuck it in the filing cabinet. It was the only place that made sense.

It took me a couple of minutes to find it since we didn't have any file folders in the cabinet yet. The papers were all lying loose in the cabinet, and I had to sift through them. Once I found them, I headed back into the main part of the store.

There, I found Maria just staring at the door, her face all puckered up as if someone had force-fed her a lemon. I raised an eyebrow. What had made her make that face?

Then, I noticed that Jesse wasn't in the shop.

"Where did he go?"

"I don't know," Maria said, clearly just as confused as me. "I turned my back on him, just for a second to put one of the purses I used in the display away. Next thing I know, I hear the door open, and he's just gone. I think his truck pulled out of the parking lot, too."

"Really?"

I groaned. Then, I did the smart thing. I put the papers down on the counter and walked out to the parking lot. Sure enough, the truck was gone. Only Maria's car remained in the parking lot. This was not good.

Had Jesse forgotten that he had given me a ride to the store? Or had he decided he didn't care?

I returned to the main area of the store. Maria raised an eyebrow.

"He's. Gone," I said through gritted teeth. "You must have heard his truck leave the parking lot. There's nothing else out there but your car. We carpooled, Jesse and I."

"I'll give you a ride home. It's all right," Maria said. "Let's see what else we can learn about our display in this packet, and then I'll get you home."

I nodded. At this point, I just wanted to curl up in my little office and make some more earrings. Maybe have a cup of hot chocolate at the side, just to keep things comfortable. It didn't really matter to me *what* I was making right now.

It'd relax me. That's all I cared about.

"All right. Let's do this, then."

With that, Maria opened the little packet. She scanned the pages, and I walked over to her as she did so. If we were going to find the answer, it might come because we were both looking at the page instead of just one of us.

"Here it is!" I smiled as I found the information we were looking for. Then, I read right from the little packet, "You're allowed to have up to two tables that could seat up to six people for a good meal – whether round or rectangular is up to you – for the merchandise. How you store extra merchandise is up to you. There will be room behind you for more, or under your tables, or in your cars."

"All right," Maria said. "How many people do you think this one would sit?"

She motioned to the one that we already had for things like this. I grabbed the small chair from the office – as we had only gotten a cheap folding chair for now – and put it at the side of the table. It took up about half of the room on one side.

"I'd say it'd fit four, comfortably," I replied.

"So, that table's fine. We need another one. Think we could score one from a thrift store if we looked hard?" Maria pursed her lips. "I don't like that we'd only have one."

"Well, it's more than enough for the jewelry. I think we'll want a larger, six-person table for all the purses if we can help it. And maybe a coat rack. I mean, think about it. We take a small piece of cardboard or wood to stick under it to keep it balanced on the grass, and we'll have a great place for extra merchandise to hang," I suggested. "And I have one that stands already. I don't use it, but it'd be great for here."

"You're right," Maria said. "Well, it's all something to think about later. Let's get you home."

I nodded. I'd been excited for this fundraiser. It was such a great opportunity to do something great for the community while also getting a boost for our new store. But I was ready to be done with having to have Jesse watching us. He wasn't doing a very good job. And I could tell he was not happy about it by the way he kept bringing up the vacation rules. It seemed that he had found a way around having to help at all with the fundraiser in past years. I wasn't sure that was a good idea now, but perhaps he should have planned a little more carefully this year.

I shook my head free of these thoughts as Maria and I walked out to the parking lot. She locked up the store, and then, we got into her car. It was a cozy little car, especially now that all the purses were out of the way.

"Something else is on your mind," Maria said as she pulled out of the parking spot. "What's going on in that head of yours?"

"Jesse disappears like that a *lot*," I responded. "He's always leaving to go do something. I wonder what he's doing. I know that he has a second job, but it sounds like he's careful about how often he goes. It's another physically demanding job. What on earth could be demanding his attention so often that he's rarely home? He must have another place to sleep..."

I pursed my lips. Though I didn't usually like to pry, this was bugging me. Something had to be going on in his life that he wasn't ready to share. As much as I was trying to respect that, I still wanted to ask all those questions.

"Well, if he's not home often, he may have a girlfriend and simply not be ready to share that with you. He may be trying to get a read on whether you'll get jealous or not before he says anything," Maria speculated. "I know a lot of men who wouldn't dare move a woman into their home unless she was their significant other."

"That's always possible. But would his girlfriend be all right with it? What if *she's* the jealous one, and telling her that he's going to be helping us out with the booth is how he's found that out?" I shook my head. "That doesn't sound quite right."

"In any case, it doesn't surprise me that he's got a house. The Delaney last name is well-known around here. I'm not sure what they did to get so well-known, but it's always been like that," Maria continued. "I don't know what he does that gives him the kind of income I think he's got, but that house is not cheap. If he's able to rent it out that low to you, either he's already paid off the mortgage, or his mortgage payments are a lot lower than the average for the area right now."

This information intrigued me.

"I could always look that information up when I get home," I said. "After all, house sales and such are public record. Usually."

"That's very true," Maria confirmed. "I hadn't thought to do that. You'll have to let me know what you find out, because now I'm curious."

I laughed a little. Maria and I were always curious, and it had been good as nurses. It didn't appear to be a good trait right now, at least when it came to Jesse. Perhaps he just wasn't used to people wondering what he was doing.

Maria dropped me off at the curb in front of the house. Jesse's truck was not in the driveway, or parked on the street. Whatever he was doing, it wasn't here. That left me alone to do a little snooping.

"Drive home safely, Maria," I said as I watched her drive off.

Then, I went inside. The first thing I did after kicking my shoes off was head upstairs to see what I could find out about the sale of this house to Jesse Delaney. My computer took a few minutes to boot up thanks to upgrades that had decided it was time to install themselves, but after that, I didn't have to search very hard to find the information I wanted.

The information about how much he paid and what the property was worth now were indeed public. I even learned what the asking price had been. What startled me was that Jesse had been able to pay almost ten thousand *more* than the asking price. It didn't appear that he had even had to take out a mortgage. That information – his mortgage and his liability for that – was not public, but what I found gave me a pretty good idea of what had happened.

"How in the world did he pay so much? And without a mortgage?" I pursed my lips after wondering this aloud. "And if he could pay that much up front, how did he get it? I didn't think being a firefighter paid that well."

I compared the price to what houses in the area were going for nowadays. He'd actually overpaid enough that the market hadn't yet caught up to the value of his house. It was close, but I wasn't sure how much longer it would be before I couldn't even afford a house at all in Lantana.

If I hadn't been jealous of Jesse Delaney for owning this house before, I certainly was now that I had looked up this information. Maybe I shouldn't have done it.

Chapter Fifteen

Fifteen: Jesse

My grip on the steering wheel only relaxed when I was at least twenty minutes away from the little shop. The traffic was not heavy today, thankfully. Perhaps my father was right. The work I did for the firehouse, as fulfilling as it was, had made me distrustful of a lot of people. I'd met so many people who would swear up and down that they would never be that kind of person. Then, I'd see them on the news for something that I would have to stop: arson, house fire, even doing something as incredibly stupid as going down into a confined space that didn't have enough oxygen.

How could they do those things after I had warned them not only of the consequences, but of the often-awful outcomes of what I had to see at work?

Though Jade expressed empathy for what I did, as I was sure she had seen some scarring burns in the hospital as a nurse, I couldn't open to her. Not for any reason.

As beautiful and sweet as she was, I couldn't risk allowing her to disappoint me too. Perhaps because if she were to disappoint me too, it would break more than my trust in her. It'd break my heart.

That thought surprised me. Why did I care so much about keeping my emotions away from Jade Santana? Why was I so afraid?

I continued to drive through Lantana, not sure where I was heading and not entirely caring. Resisting the urge to drive all the way to the ranch, I made another left turn to continue around the block for now. Though I knew the ranch would allow me to work through the frustrations without anyone questioning why I was hitting the dirt with the hoe so hard, or why I was happy to do some of the dirtiest jobs, there just wasn't enough time for that to be applicable tonight.

Especially since I had a feeling that the chief would be watching closely to be sure that I actually helped. He had expressed his wishes to see me help with the fundraiser before, but I had never wanted to.

After an hour of riding around and thinking about the situation, I decided that it was time to head home. There were a few reasons – the growling in my stomach being one of them – but the main reason that the sky looked as though it was going to start pouring rain. That was the last thing that I wanted to have to drive through right now.

I arrived home safely, and was not entirely shocked to see that Jade's car was there. We had carpooled after all. I checked my phone. She hadn't called to see if I could come give her a ride home... perhaps that meant that she had gone to Maria's for a while, and Maria would be bringing her home.

But when I went to open the front door, I found it unlocked. Jade was home. She had to be. Otherwise, the door would be locked. I sighed softly before walking into the living room and shutting the front door behind me.

I kicked my shoes off. There was a soft vanilla scent in the air. Perhaps she had lit a candle. Though I wasn't usually much for scented candles, I had to admit that this one was nice.

The further I got into the home, the more I wondered where Jade was. She was not in the living room or the dining room, which were the two rooms that I could easily see from the entry way. If she was not in there, was she in the kitchen and baking with vanilla extract instead of having lit a candle?

Turning the corner, I found her coming out of the laundry room. She had started laundry while I was gone and switched it, probably. Or had just started it. Who knew?

"Welcome back, Jesse," she said.

Her tone worried me a little bit. It was hard, icy. As if she was determined to be as warm with me as I was with her. For some reason I had not anticipated, it hurt.

"Thanks. I'm... sorry for leaving you without a ride at the store. I just need to, uh, to clear my head," I said.

Hopefully she'd recognize that I didn't want to share the real reason with her, or she would take the lie at face value. She only nodded. Whatever it meant to her, she was going to keep it to herself.

She walked right past me. I let her. However, since my stomach would not shut up, I went into the kitchen. I started filling a pot with some water as she sat down at the counter.

"Would... would you like some ravioli?" I glanced at Jade as I was filling the pot.

I only had one pot for noodles. It was a large three-quart pot that would easily make enough ravioli for the both of us if we needed to do that.

"No."

I put the pot on the stove and turned on the burner before turning the water off. Jade was still standing in the doorway.

"And I'll tell you what else," she continued. She sounded terrifyingly calm. "I'm sick of the way that you've been treating me. Our interactions are painfully awkward because I don't know what to say to you that won't end in you either deciding to walk away or getting upset with me and yelling at me about how hard it is to be a firefighter."

Her voice shook a little, and I wondered how long she had been working up the courage to say anything to me. How long she had wanted to say something and hadn't been sure if I would react in a way that she'd regret.

"Not only that, but the words you said to me in the store about my jewelry were hurtful. I know my jewelry is not everyone's cup of tea," she continued, not giving me a chance to say anything. "I just don't understand why you've decided that I'm the perfect punching bag for your frustrations. Go to the gym! Go out on a drive. Do something else, *anything* else than yell at me again for just trying to get to know the man I'm sharing a house with."

I felt my ears turn hot. I had a feeling she was right, but I couldn't find the words to admit it. "I don't want to talk about it. It's absolutely none of your business how I decide to take my frustrations out."

I turned back to face the pot of water. While a watched pot never boiled, it was far more exciting than facing Jade.

Perhaps renting out the upstairs had been a terrible idea. But she was here now, and hadn't done anything to break her lease. As much as I wanted her out of the house, I knew that I didn't have any legal grounds to kick her out. If she brought up breaking her lease, then I would let her without any penalties and take the place off the market. It was not worth the trouble.

"You're making it my business by always being angry at me," Jade retorted bitterly. "Even now, while I'm trying to have a productive conversation with you about it all, you're shutting me down as if my opinion has absolutely no bearing on what is going on in the house. I wondered why a man like you would have such a large house and no family. The upstairs would be perfect for your children to run around in, play in, but you seem to be capable of turning everyone you meet against you just by speaking to them. And I don't understand it! What have I done to you to deserve this kind of anger?"

I clenched my fist and counted to ten. Maybe I should have gone to the ranch instead of coming home.

"Jade, I have been a firefighter for ten years," I started, but my voice rose to a yell quickly. "I have lost friends, fellow firefighters, and plenty of other people I didn't even know in this line of work. Each and every one of them, I visited in the hospital! The burns on their bodies haunt me, and I cannot take getting close to anyone else. Do you know how awful it is to see a building and only think about how it would go up in a blaze and decide whether you'd occupy it based on that alone or not? How much time I spend thinking about how each building's sprinklers work, praying that they're connected right to buy everyone time to get out and suppress the fire so everyone can get out before the fire department gets there?"

Both of my hands were clenched tight in fists at my sides, and though I could hear the water in the pot bubbling furiously now, I didn't much care for dinner.

"So, you'll have to excuse me if I come off a little stand-offish because I refuse to lose another person I don't know very well to the memories of the hospital and the burns and the awful cries of pain because there are some kinds of burns that you just can't numb! And, I'll be honest, I don't much appreciate that you're using the same colors of fire for the beads in the jewelry that you're going to be selling. How dare you make a mockery of what we do by using the same colors that haunt all of us to raise money for us to do our jobs."

Jade's mouth hung open. I hoped she had nothing more to say, and I pulled the ravioli out of the freezer and put a few of the pieces in the water. My appetite had significantly shrunk upon getting accosted with these claims. I pushed her away for her own good. For *my* own good. If she were to get hurt, and I were to have to visit her in the hospital... I didn't want to know how I'd react to it.

I set a timer on the microwave.

"You're not the only person who's ever lost someone. You're not the only person who's ever seen hard things. And no one owns the color red, *Mr. Delaney*."

I didn't look at her.

The quiet in the kitchen now was tenuous. It was far worse than the silence before Jade had accused me of being angry at her for no reason. I had every reason to be angry that she was using red, yellow, and orange beads. Those colors were not in my wardrobe for a reason, and I was sure many of the other firefighters at the station would back me up on this one.

As beautiful as they were – color wise and in the beads that allowed the sun to shine through them, they were *gorgeous* – I could not look at them the same way I had before I had become a fire fighter. Where they were once the color of a sunrise to me, they now symbolized all of the fires I had gone through – the scars on my arms and the one on my back surely spoke of the troubles I'd had with my gear in my early years – and the pain, the struggles that came with them. The memories of the firefighters who had given their lives to ensure the rest of us made it out of a particularly dangerous fire were always what came back to me when I saw those colors together.

The odd thing was that I could handle them on their own.

The timer beeped, pulling me out of my thoughts. I strained the noodles, and added some pasta sauce to the plate once the ravioli settled. I pulled a fork out of the silverware drawer. The last thing I wanted to do right now was eat in the kitchen, so I went into the dining room.

Perhaps it would have been better to walk into my room, but something about the way Jade sat melancholically staring at the pot made me wonder if she had only refused the ravioli because I was making it and she hadn't wanted to risk making me mad at her while I was making her food.

I started eating quietly. The ravioli was filled with ricotta, mozzarella, and a couple of other cheeses. While there was a meat and cheese version, I preferred this one. Something about the cheese just sat better with me than it did when meat was added to it. Didn't know why, didn't entirely care. It was good food.

That was all that mattered.

About halfway through my food, Jade walked into the dining room.

Chapter Sixteen

Sixteen: Jade

I wasn't particularly shocked to hear about the things Jesse had lost. He'd mentioned many of those things before. I was shocked by his saying he was mean because he "refused to lose another person." What did he mean by that? Did he mean he didn't want to lose me?

"What do you want?" Jesse asked, his voice harsh and insincere.

"I didn't mean to push you like that," I started. "But, I'm just trying to understand. You're the only firefighter who is not happy about any of the fundraising. The rest of the crews seem super excited that we're there to help them raise the money needed to replace gear, get the fire house fixed up, all of that. Whatever you all decide to use the money for, I just want to help raise that money."

He simply took his half-finished plate of ravioli and stood up.

"I don't want to hear any more on this subject."

With that, he walked away and into his bedroom, slamming the door for extra measure.

"I-I…"

I sighed. Whatever this man was trying to get across, I didn't know. But I did know that my stomach was going to start growling soon enough. Maybe if I made something to share, it would build a small bridge.

In the kitchen, I pulled out a pan and then some strips of chicken. It was time to sear this up because otherwise, it was going to go bad. And I didn't want to waste that kind of money. Not after such a big move.

As I cooked the chicken, I took care in cutting up some peppers and a few other toppings. Fajitas were a comfort food of mine, and after all that had happened today, I think I needed that. Besides, with Jesse being as stand-offish as he was today, I didn't want to take the chance and make myself some ravioli from his bag. As good as it had smelled with the sauce that he had put on it, it wasn't worth making him *angrier* at me.

"If only I could figure out why he's always so angry at me," I muttered as I finished cutting up the vegetables I would be searing as well.

I washed off the knife and the cutting board I had used. Then, I grabbed my phone. Usually, I'd play music while I cooked, but I felt more like I needed to talk to someone. Instead of a phone conversation, though, I texted Maria.

Jesse is super stand-offish today. Apparently the color of beads I use is offensive or something. Ugh what do I have to do to get my landlord to stop yelling at me?

With that, I then realized that it was raining hard outside. Jesse had probably gone to his room instead of leaving the house because he didn't want to get poured on outside. I quietly hoped the power would remain on through the intense storm outside. We were out of hurricane season, but that didn't mean that we couldn't have large storms in Texas.

Jesse only came out momentarily to put his plate in the sink.

"Do you want a fajita or two for tomorrow?" I asked, attempting to make some light conversation that had no bearing on anything else going on around us.

He gave me no answer. Instead, he simply walked back to his room. This time, the door didn't slam. I was thankful that he was no longer slamming the doors, but the fact that he had straight-up ignored me hurt more than the slamming door made my ears hurt. It felt so childish, storming off and slamming doors and giving people the silent treatment. Did he realize how that could impact our relationship as landlord and tenant? And if so, was he hoping that it would inspire me to move out?

I shook my head. That was the last thing I needed to be thinking of right now. What I wanted to think about was actually rather simple. I wanted to be thinking about the fajitas and about texting Maria. If this didn't work out with Jesse, we needed to have another plan for who we would be working with come the day of the fundraiser.

Once the chicken was all cooked, I quickly fried the vegetables in another pan. I added everything to a warm tortilla, and sat down at the table with my phone, which vibrated softly in my hand.

"All right, Maria. What do you say?"

I opened my phone and found that it was not a response from Maria, but from Jesse. I raised an eyebrow. Why would he be messaging me instead of just coming out to talk to me?

I need some time. Fajitas for tomorrow sound great.

I now wondered if he hadn't been ignoring me, but had decided that he needed to isolate himself from me for a little while. I felt like I needed to reply. Instead of words, I simply sent him a thumbs up in response. I could make sure I put aside stuff for fajitas for tomorrow's lunch.

Thanks.

His reply was swift. I pursed my lips.

If I texted him, would we have a better chance at having a productive conversation? It wasn't something I was willing to test out tonight, but it was something I needed to keep in mind. Certainly, it'd have the same kind of impact if I sent the wrong words put together.

I shook my head and began to eat my fajitas.

Once I was done with dinner, I put the rest of the vegetables and chicken into a plastic container to be put in the fridge. Then, I put my tortillas away. At least it sounded like Jesse was willing to talk to me. I wondered if he just needed an hour or two to compose himself after I pushed his buttons, accidentally.

So, I pressed on with my original plan. I made some cookies. This recipe mixed together quite easily, honestly, but it was the baking and spooning it all out that took longer. It made delicious chocolate chip cookies, though. He didn't want any of the dough, and I knew that. However, I did take a little bit, just to make sure that it was good and as it should be.

What kind of a baker would I be if I didn't at least taste the dough to make sure it had come together right?

After I put the first batch of cookies in the oven, I checked my phone to see if anyone had texted me. There was nothing from Jesse, which I had suspected would be the case. However, there was something from Maria.

Whatever the case, he's always like that. Is it worse tonight?

Maria was at least giving him the benefit of the doubt. I sighed softly. She deserved to know that I had pushed his buttons, but I didn't think that I had said anything that would have set him off like that. Perhaps it was because he hadn't known what to say about the color combinations I'd decided to use and had let it fester until he didn't have any choice *but* to say something. If that was the case, I didn't want to know what he would do if he didn't like the ideas I was seeing in my head for how to replace the color combinations.

I didn't know how to answer Maria, so I sat on her text.

The first batch of cookies finished, and I put in another sheet. I could smell the first ones that had come out. They had cooked beautifully. The edges were a little brown, but not a burnt brown. A golden-brown that meant they were just right.

That was all I wanted to see.

I put a couple cookies on a plate to cool before having one myself, straight out of the oven. While it was still unbearably hot, the chocolate especially, it was one of the best feelings in the world.

I glanced at the kitchen window as I enjoyed the cookie. The rain was coming down in torrents. It almost looked like a full sheet of rain drops descending from the sky. There were full puddles forming on the ground that I could see, and I decided that I wasn't going to go anywhere tonight. Perhaps if it wasn't raining, I would have gone to get some sugar cookies.

Once all of the cookies had come out of the oven, I took the ones I had originally put on a plate and headed for the master bedroom. The oven was off, as I always turned it off when I was done. Habit.

I knocked on the door. Jesse had not texted me since I had given him a thumbs up on the fajitas for tomorrow, but I hoped that he would not mind the interruption for the sweet treat of freshly made cookies.

He opened the door, glaring at me. He appeared ready to chew me out for daring to knock on the door until he saw the cookies.

"I'm sorry," I said quickly before he could slam the door. I held the cookies up for him to take. "I just came with a peace offering. Have one, or all of them. I have plenty more in the kitchen."

He looked me straight in the eye and I suddenly noticed how clear they were. I felt my stomach do a weird flip thing. He sighed, looked at his shoes, then looked back at me.

"I should be the one apologizing," he admitted before taking a cookie. "It wasn't right of me to yell at you like that. I've had some... anger issues that I've been working on, and I messed up tonight... probably more than just tonight."

That was as specific as he got, but it gave me some insight into what he was dealing with. I'd had no idea he struggled with anger. Perhaps it was just something he was telling me to give me an explanation for what had happened without having to be vulnerable with me. Truly vulnerable, at least. I didn't want to pry.

So, I decided to take the anger issue excuse at face value. At least it meant that I might not be the problem, which was a relief. You can only be yelled at so many times before you begin to wonder if you might just be a terrible person to be around.

"Well, if you think you'd be able to handle it, I wanted to show you the designs I want to use for the fundraiser. I think getting a firefighter's opinion on the colors and designs would be a good idea, since there will be so many around," I said.

His mouth was full of cookie, so he only nodded.

With that, I moved so that he could go to the dining room table. It seemed that he had no intention of joining me upstairs, which is what I had originally hoped he'd do.

"Let me grab everything from upstairs," I said. "It might take me a minute to get everything."

"Make the trip safely," Jesse said.

It was the first time he'd said anything about safety to me. And I chose to believe that this was the start of a turning point in our relationship. Perhaps we wouldn't end up being good friends, as I had originally hoped we would, but this at least meant that he was learning to open up to me. That I generally meant him no harm. What harm came about was because we couldn't seem to communicate to save our lives.

I quickly hurried upstairs. There, I gathered the bracelets and earrings I had finished. I also grabbed my sketch book and my colored pencils. Sometimes, the best way to see a design was to sketch it out before I started putting beads together.

Chapter Seventeen

Seventeen: Jesse

When Jade returned, I had finished my cookie. I appreciated that she had made something, but I hoped she hadn't felt like she'd had to bake something in order to talk to me. However, when she started setting everything down on the table, I wondered why she had brought both actual jewelry and what she had sketched. Was she hoping that she could find another color scheme if I was sitting beside her? Helping her with the colors?

As much as I appreciated that she might have been on that path, I was learning that I needed to stop assuming things about Jade. So, I waited patiently for her to say anything about what she had brought down.

"Sorry," she started. "I can be a little scatter-brained. As long as the clients don't know that I'm this scatter-brained, they don't realize just how much work goes into what I create. Now, here are some of the ones I've already made. And I'm hoping that we could come up with some better color schemes together. I'd hate for all of the fire fighters to be struggling to get a look at my booth. They all looked rather intrigued when we shared that we sell exclusively hand-made items."

I looked at the jewelry she had brought down. It seemed that she had decided to tone down the beading for these because they were rather simple designs. These looked a lot better than the designs she had had on display in the shop.

"I already like the simplistic designs better," I said. "I think jewelry looks best when it's simple, and it accents your beauty or outfit instead of being so loud that all you can look at is the jewelry."

Jade looked at me, her eyebrow raised. However, there was a hint of a blush on her cheeks that I noticed. Unbidden, I noted how pretty her face looked. I shook myself, I needed to stay focused. I owed it to her. Especially after I had practically blown up at her over asking me questions. I needed to show her that I respected her. Respect, after all, was given freely if it had been earned.

I hoped I would earn her respect if I showed her that I was willing to respect her feelings in the way I wished mine to be respected.

"How did you come to that conclusion?" she asked.

"I've met a lot of women who believe that the jewelry they wear should be the only thing you look at in an outfit – whether that's a ring, a necklace, a bracelet, earrings, a watch, or some combination thereof – because it'll keep a man's eyes off of the rest of the outfit."

"Well," Jade smiled. It was a good smile. "Women tend to dress for themselves. If a woman you know has taken precautions to make sure eyes are drawn to her wrists or her neck instead of somewhere else, you should probably let her make that choice and not ask questions about why she's decided that's the best practice," Jade started. "But, I'm glad you like the simplistic designs. I do, too. I thought they suited this idea better than the ones I usually do. And doing some earrings shaped like tiny flames felt like a bad idea to me."

I nodded slowly. I guess she hadn't really wanted to glorify fire with her jewelry. Tiny flames on earrings felt like a good idea if she was raising money for fire awareness. Something along the lines of 'here's a fire you can touch' teaching with children.

"How long does it take you to make a pair of earrings like this?" I held up one of the earrings she had brought down.

It was clearly for those with pierced ears, as the post was more of a clamp that happened to go through the hole in the ear. Much like antique earrings, I supposed. I wondered why she had chosen to make it like this instead of adding a simple post on the back. Then again, this earring was somewhat heavy in my hand. Maybe a post wouldn't have held the weight of the earring very well at all, while this clamp-like design seemed sturdier. It couldn't fall out easily.

"It takes me about an hour to bead a pair like that," she revealed. "I could even do it just watching television. The biggest labor piece with those is sewing them to the felt and making sure I leave enough room for the posts." She shrugged. "I don't make them very often because I prefer to stock unique pieces. But for a fundraiser where I don't have time to make the unique pieces, these work well enough. I can make a lot while you're away."

I nodded slowly.

The bracelets and necklaces she had available for me to look at on the table all had strands of single colors. Either the bracelets were sold as a set, or she was planning to sell them separately. Some of the necklaces looked as though they were actually a fire burning with the effect of the light coming through the glass. It was unnerving to me.

"What's your favorite design? I could use that again, but with different colors," Jade said as I continued looking. "These glass beads always look so pretty against the skin. The skin, depending on what color it is, can darken the colors or make them a little lighter. Either way, they shine brilliantly under most lighting."

I nodded slowly at that remark. I could see why she would be using the glass beads for the fundraiser, then.

"I think these are," I said as I pulled the bracelet, necklace, and earring that I liked most out of the chaos around us. "They're simple but really pretty. You know, if you did them in hues of blue and green, with a little bit of red and black at either end, you could say they were modeled off the hoses we use."

"That's... that's actually a great idea. It's a subtle enough design, especially on a necklace where those extra colors are up by the clasp, that not everyone would immediately understand it's supposed to be a fire hose." She smiled a little. "Thanks for that idea. What about for the colors in general? I... I want this to be easy for the fire fighters – all of them – to come look at."

"From what I've heard, the firefighters who attend the fundraiser are usually there to make sure it runs smoothly and are too busy to look anywhere but the problems they've been presented with or the booth they've been assigned to run," I mentioned. "Unless you're going to make problems the day of the fundraiser, I think I spoke too soon."

Jade looked up at me, her eyes wide. She seemed quite confused that I was able to admit that I had done something wrong. While it wasn't something I did often, I could indeed admit when I was wrong. At the very least, I had to admit it to myself to fix mistakes that I made while alone. Otherwise, it was just to make sure that I was doing things right.

"Well, well. It seems you are capable of change, Jesse Delaney," she teased me with a bit of a smirk. "I'm glad to know that. Now, I say we put on a movie in the living room. I can bead while we watch, and you can watch the movie or draw or whatever it is that puts your mind at ease. That storm sounds like it's going to be raging for a while, and I don't want to go anywhere in the rain tonight."

I pursed my lips. This felt oddly vulnerable, but instead of walking to my room, I nodded.

"Let me grab my phone. I like to play word games while I watch movies."

She raised an eyebrow, but all the same, she took her finished jewelry back upstairs as I went to make sure I had a phone charger at the ready. The games I liked to play drained my battery immensely. It was always better to play them plugged in, if I could help it.

When I went out to the living room, Jade had set up a large table in the living room beside the arm of the couch. It appeared to be the same table I had stored in the pantry when I had first seen it. When she opened the top of it to reveal a felt pad for her to work on, I now realized why she was so mad that it had ended up in the pantry. This was where she did all her beading.

If food had gotten onto that felt pad, it might have ended badly for the jewelry she had in there. I didn't think she had moved it with beads in there, but I could have been wrong.

"If you get any food, it has to stay *off* this table," Jade warned me. "This is a beading table. It's not meant for food, and I have seen food stain my glass beads before. Understand?"

"I understand, Jade."

With that, we turned on a comedy that we had both seen a million times. What intrigued me the most was that she was able to recite the lines, in the right intonations, as she was beading. It seemed she had done this before, and she had suggested this because it was something that could put us both at ease.

I turned to my phone. It had actually died during dinner, so I was out of luck for now. Instead of fussing about it, I plugged it into the cord I kept out here and put it on the armrest of the chair. Then, I turned to watch the movie. Except, I had a clearer view of what Jade was doing to make her jewelry than the television.

I really needed to rearrange the furniture in here one day soon.

"How long have you been beading, Jade? In general?" I asked as the curiosity overtook me.

Her hands moved as if she had done this a thousand times. It was perhaps a good thing I could recognize the expertise, but I had to know what the answer was.

"I've been consistently beading for... I'd say about ten years," she admitted. "I made extra money in nursing school this way. Not a lot, since I didn't have consistent inventory, but enough that I was able to at least afford textbooks with the profits most semesters. After nursing school, I decided to try and make a better business out of it to pay off my debts. It worked."

"That's quite resourceful of you," I said.

Jade nodded, not once looking up from the work she was doing. It looked like she was working on a pair of earrings, judging by the size of the felt in her hands that she was sewing the beads to. She picked the beads up on a sewing needle from the felt on the table, which I thought was a genius way to do it so long as she didn't draw blood with the needle.

I turned my attention back to the movie. She was clearly deeply involved in her work, and I didn't want to be the reason she couldn't finish at least one pair of earrings tonight to add to the bag of jewelry she was going to be selling for the fundraiser.

Instead of paying attention to the movie, or to my game, I found myself continually glancing over at Jade. Something about her mesmerized me.

Chapter Eighteen

Eighteen: Jade

Even though I got the feeling that this is not how he preferred to make his friends, I appreciated that Jesse was attempting to get to know me through what I did to make money. It may not have been the same as saving people in a fire, but it was my thing. Just as fighting fires and running elsewhere when he wasn't on shift were his.

"So, I don't do this very often, but you look like the kind of man who is utterly lost on what to give a woman," I said. I didn't know how else I was going to do this, and I knew that if I *didn't* say something, the idea that he had a girlfriend was going to destroy me. I had to know. "If you want, I could make you a bracelet to give to a special someone."

"Oh, um…" Jesse's face flushed a little.

I raised an eyebrow. That was honestly not the kind of response I had expected. Instead, I had expected him to either get on my case about assuming things about him, or for him to stay silent. For him to mutter, hem, and haw at me was new. Unusual. I appreciated it.

"I'm not dating anyone currently," he finally said.

I felt an unbidden smile start to warm my face.

"And I don't plan to do so for a long while. But thank you for the offer."

I felt vaguely disappointed.

His voice took a gentle tone this time. Whomever had last dated him must have seen the kind of man he was when he wasn't all angry at the world, and I wondered if I was starting to see beneath that exterior gruffness. This wasn't a man who was determined to make the world go away. Instead, Jesse Delaney appeared to be shielding himself. From what, I didn't know.

And I wasn't sure I wanted to know.

"Oh. I'm sorry if I touched a nerve."

I didn't press any further. He deserved his privacy.

"It's not your fault." Jesse let out a soft sigh. "I suppose there's nothing more to say, but I think you deserve to know why. It's... it's part of why I've been struggling to open up to you. To talk to you. A few years ago, I answered a call for firefighters at the station. The address... it sounded familiar, but I didn't place it until I was standing there with a hose hooked up to the hydrant that this was my best friend's home."

"Did... did they make it?"

Jesse only shook his head.

"I'm so sorry."

I put my beading supplies down, thinking that Jesse's mental anguish was far more important than some pair of earrings right now. They could wait.

As I turned to look at Jesse, he had turned his face away from me. I wondered why. Perhaps he subscribed to the idea that it wasn't manly to be seen crying, but this was the loss of a friend he clearly hadn't dealt with very well yet. I didn't think that there was anything wrong with him to be mourning a friend so dearly. After all, the tone in which he spoke about his friend told me all I needed to know.

They had been close, and this death had been incredibly hard for him to process.

"Is there anything I can do to make it a little easier?" I offered.

I knew there probably wasn't much, but I wasn't sure what else to do. If I didn't offer, it looked horrible. If I did, at least he knew that I was trying to do something to help him through this.

He shook his head.

"No." His tone remained unusually even. "It was a few years ago. Talking about it still hurts, but I have processed much of the grief... I think. It just shattered me. Couldn't work for a few months after that. Not at the station, anyway."

I walked over to where he sat and put my hand on his shoulder, gently. He may not like that I was more of the touchy-feely type, but he clearly needed the support. Even if he was still struggling with how to go on with his life without this friend, he had made a path for himself. I only had to wonder if it made him happy at all.

"Are you happy with how your life has turned out since your friend's death?"

The shocked silence that sat between us said it all to me. He may not have known what he wanted out of life, but I didn't think he was getting anywhere in life with how he was acting. Perhaps I was wrong. But there was nothing more obvious about his life than the fact that he appeared to be stuck in a rut.

"Why do you ask that?" Jesse asked, finally turning to face me.

He wasn't tearful, as I had thought he might be. Instead, his face was simply pale. This topic was clearly hard for him to stomach. Something that made a firefighter queasy was nothing to laugh at.

"Because I've had plenty of time to notice what you do when you're home," I replied. "Jesse, you kind of live in a rut. You have the same foods for each meal that I've seen you cook, and it all seems to come out of a bag or box. The only thing you're really doing is making sure that you get calories. I suppose that's a good thing, but you don't appear to *enjoy* life. At all."

Jesse simply shrugged.

"I was like this before his death, too," he revealed. "I never really saw a need to cook a lot of food at four-thirty in the morning. I eat a small breakfast here, have a better one at the fire station later in the day, and lunch and dinner are all foods that could easily fill me up so that I can go."

"I see."

I moved back to the couch now. There was nothing more to say about his habits. If he was happy with them, then I didn't think it was worth bugging him about them any longer.

"Do you ever visit them? I mean, like their grave?" I didn't want to overstep, but he hadn't shut me out so far.

He shook his head.

"If you wanted, I could make you something that you could leave there—I guess that would make more sense if your friend's a woman. Or we could get flowers or something for them? Or a picture of their favorite animal or something?" I glanced at Jesse. "I'm not entirely sure what else to suggest, but I think it'd be... a sweet... gesture..."

As I trailed off into the end of the movie, Jesse simply walked out of the room. I didn't follow after him. The fact that he was not yelling at me to stop talking or suggesting that I needed to take a page from his book and mind my own business was a good sign, but I worried that I had crossed a line all the same. I'd taken his nod as a willingness to continue the conversation, but maybe I'd misread him.

I sat back on the couch, sighing softly. Shortly after this, I heard the sounds of the front door opening, shutting, and locking. It sounded as though Jesse meant to be out for a while, since he had locked the door. That, or it was his habit to lock the door every time he left the house.

"Oh, Jesse Delaney. You're a mystery," I muttered. "I'll figure you out soon enough. I promise you that."

I shook my head before turning off the movie and putting on one of the many TV shows I watched while I was beading. If Jesse was going to let me have the living room all to myself, then it was only fair that I got to watch something that would allow me to focus more on my beading than the conversation I was having with him.

Especially now that he was no longer in the room.

However, the part of the conversation that stuck out the most to me was that he was not dating anyone. Maria had been wrong in that regard. If that was the case, then when he wasn't here or at the fire station, where did he go? He had talked about having a second job, but surely that wasn't *all* he did. If that was, then he was the epitome of a workhorse.

And I didn't know how I felt about sharing a home with someone like that. At least, not in the long term. While I was just trying to get on my feet in Lantana, it would be fine. Perhaps even if I ended up working as a nurse here because I'd be equally as exhausted when I got home, if that was the case.

Instead of dwelling on what he did when he wasn't home, I focused on my beading.

I ended up creating quite a few pairs of earrings. Enough that I had to bring more supplies down from my supply upstairs. For half a second, I thought about moving everything upstairs instead of just taking my supplies down, but I decided that the larger screen in the living room was worth it. While I could have easily watched these things on my desktop, it was more fun working in the living room every now and then.

To be honest, I kind of missed the feeling of staying up late into the night just beading on my little table. I had done it so many times before I moved, partially out of necessity and partially to stay ahead of the orders on my site.

Instead of entirely beading for the fundraiser, since I'd have time when I staffed the store to do that between customers, I focused on making things for the customers who were ordering online or coming into the store. Then, I texted Maria with an idea that came courtesy of something on the show that I was watching.

What if we get a tablet, have it set up to look at the website I run, and let customers browse the online stuff there too? More sales that way, I'd think.

I put my phone back on the beading table and continued to work on the long trails of beads needed for this particular pair of earrings. I never really understood the appeal of wearing earrings so long they touched one's shoulders. However, they were all the rage right now. And they were ridiculously easy to make, compared to some of the other styles I made. Some of them had some felt to keep them from getting tangled, but others were loose to let the beads dangle and swing.

Eventually, my fingers felt the pain of having beaded too much for a day. I put everything back in the table, closing the top. I could get that back upstairs tomorrow, since I didn't have much else to do before I was supposed to be at the store. Besides, it was late and Maria probably wouldn't respond about the tablet idea until the morning.

As I moved to go upstairs, I felt the cool air hit me. The rain had really made the temperature drop, and the idea of crawling into a cold bed was not appealing. I turned back to look at the warm couch.

I walked to the little powder room. After using it and washing my hands and face, I let out a heck of a yawn. Whatever time it was now,

I had a feeling that Jesse wasn't going to be coming back until the morning. Perhaps that was why he had locked the door.

So, instead of attempting to get myself up the stairs and make a cozy nest in my own room, I made my way back to the couch and laid down. I closed my eyes as I listened to the rain pattering against the window. It was so peaceful.

Chapter Nineteen

Nineteen: Jesse

After I shut the front door, I locked it with shaky hands. I leaned against the side of the doorframe, trying to calm my racing heart. Tears welled in my eyes for what felt like the first time in forever. Since my friend's death, it had been the same routine. Go to the fire station. Go to the ranch. If I had anything else to do – errands, training, whatever it was – I did it before going to the ranch. I clung to that routine for dear life.

But I hadn't been to my friend's grave since the funeral. Couldn't stomach it. The thought that I would never be able to talk to him again had hurt so much after that fire. To know that Jade had some kind of empathy – something I'd not seen in many months – had almost broken me right in front of her.

I walked to my truck. It wouldn't do me any good, right now, to start sobbing in front of her. She saw me as this irrationally angry man. As much as I didn't want that to be her image of me, I couldn't blame her for it. After losing my friend, I had started withdrawing from everyone. Even my father had noticed it, though he assumed it was because of my job just as my brothers had become jaded.

As I hopped into the front seat, I took in a deep breath. Willing the tears away so that I could drive, I decided that perhaps Jade was right. Even if it wasn't a beaded bracelet left at the grave, I needed to do something. Leave something to tell him that I was still visiting.

Though it was late, I headed to the grocery store. They would have a decent-ish selection of flowers, I supposed. Even though I knew that, at this time of year, I could go pick a sunflower off the side of the road if I really wanted to. He'd always pointed out the sunflowers when we drove down the highway together. This grocery store sold sunflowers. At least, during the summer. I hoped I wasn't too late to be able to buy one.

The grocery store was mostly empty, probably because of the rain. Upon arriving at the small selection of bouquets and fresh flowers, I found a small bouquet of sunflowers. They were starting to wilt, but they'd do for what I wanted. I grabbed the little bouquet. Then, I made my way to the register.

The woman working the register appeared to be ready to go home. She wasn't entirely talkative, but gave me the total as she should have. I paid, and then returned to the truck.

"Here goes nothing, I guess."

I took in a deep breath as I headed towards the cemetery. Whatever Jade's intentions had been, I was quietly thankful for the reminder that it was all right to visit the grave again. Most around here didn't visit the graves of the fallen, no matter how close they were. Unless it was a family member, at least. I wished that it was treated differently. However, there was nothing more I could do for that.

When I arrived at the cemetery, I parked my truck and walked with the sunflowers to my friend's grave. To my surprise, I found someone had actually planted a sunflower at his grave. Perhaps his parents. The rain soaked through my jacket quickly, but all I could think about was how good the rain would be for the plant. .

I placed the bouquet of sunflowers on the wet grass beside the headstone.

"I miss you," I whispered.

The tears returned to my eyes, mixing with the rain. I sniffled a little. How could one simple little visit have me in tears?

I let them flow this time, wondering if perhaps this is exactly what I needed to stop being so snappy with Jade. She didn't deserve any of the frustration I'd unleashed on her, especially since she was only trying to help. I knew I owed her an apology, along with a giant thanks for tolerating how I had been and helping me see how to straighten it all out. It certainly wouldn't happen in one day.

But she had started something that I meant to finish.

I knelt down on the dirt beside the headstone, ignoring the mud as the tears ran down my cheeks as the sun began to set. The conversation with Jade had also given me something that I had not felt in a long time. For so long, I had only confided in Henry – my friend who now lay in the ground beside me – because he would never judge me for the emotions I felt. He had a way of listening that made me feel seen.

No one else had found a way to listen to me and make me feel as seen and understood as he had... until tonight. Until talking to Jade, I realized that she had taken the time to listen not just to the words I spoke, but to look at my body language, my tone, all of it. And in that, she had found a message I hadn't even been aware I was trying to convey.

Once the sobs had passed, and I had managed to calm myself down enough, I decided that it was time to give Jade a small insight into what I did every day. I knew that she was curious. She'd asked about it before. It seemed that she wanted to know where I disappeared to that kept me away from the home for days at a time if I wasn't at the fire station. I didn't even know why I'd kept it so secret. I guess that, after Henry, treating anyone like a friend felt dangerous. All I could think was 'what if I lose them too?'

As I slowly walked back to the truck, I decided that it was time for half the truth to come out. As much as I wanted to share everything with her – about my family's wealth, that I was working as a fire fighter because I wanted to help people and stop disasters from getting worse – I knew that it was not yet time to share all of that. If she reacted well to the fact that I still went to a place from my childhood, then I would think about what her reaction to everything else would be.

But I couldn't reveal my wealth to just anyone. I wanted my friends to like me for *me;* my personality, my speech, my morals. I hadn't showcased any of those very well in the past few weeks with Jade, but I wanted to do better.

I suddenly realized that I cared very much that Jade came to like me for who I was.

As I drove home, my stomach started to knot up. After the way Jade had yelled at me, I wasn't sure that she'd be open to this conversation. Tonight, anyway. I supposed there was only one way to find out what she thought of it all, and that required having a conversation.

I glanced at the clock on my radio.

It was just past ten in the evening. She probably wasn't asleep yet. And if she was, then I'd have to wait until tomorrow morning to have the conversation with her.

I could wait that long if needed.

The drive home was not as difficult as the drive out to the cemetery or to the grocery store as the rain was beginning to let up. Also perhaps because I had let out the tears that made it difficult to see. Or because

I was no longer entirely emotional over everything. Whatever the case was, I was glad for it.

When I arrived, I pulled my keys out of my pocket. My hands no longer shook. At least I had made some progress, I supposed.

I walked in and quietly shut and locked the door behind me.

The living room light was still on, though, which confused me just a little bit. I walked into the living room. There, I found Jade's beading table neatly put away against the arm of the couch. It appeared that all of her beads were contained within. A few of the pieces she had made were on top, perhaps to let the glue she used dry without worrying about it sticking to other beads if it got hit.

I was about to turn off the lights when I noticed that Jade was fast asleep on the couch. A small smile tugged at my lips. Our conversation could certainly wait until tomorrow now. There was no way I was waking her up after the evening we'd had. Instead, I grabbed one of the blankets I kept under the coffee table and draped it over her sleeping form.

Her head was turned to the side, so I quietly closed all the curtains. Thankfully, they were on automatic tracks. All I had to do was press a button to close them all. Once the curtains were closed, I turned off the lights in the living room.

I knew this house like the back of my hand. With a hand trailing on the wall, just to make sure that I didn't miss my door, I walked down the hallway to go into the master bedroom. Once I found the knob, I entered my room and turned on the lamps with a flick of the switch. It didn't take long for me to change out of my clothes and into a pair of sweatpants and an old T-shirt to sleep in.

As I lay down on the bed, I wasn't entirely sure what I was going to do in the morning, but I had a feeling that Jade would be awake before me. I hadn't blocked her into the driveway, as I had parked on the curb. However, there was nothing more I could do right now.

As I fell asleep, I quietly thanked Jade for the push she had given me to go see my friend's grave.

The next morning, I showered after I woke up. My face felt hot and flushed, but I supposed it was only because of the tears I had cried the night before. After a shower, I felt much better. I did get a glass of water from the tap in the bathroom, just to be safe.

Then, I got dressed. Just a simple pair of shorts and a T-shirt. Nothing fancy. I wasn't going anywhere today. I had an unusually empty morning, and I realized I hadn't had one of those in a long time. I had no plans to rush off to the ranch, and I wasn't working at the station until later.

When I went out to see if Jade was awake, I found her still fast asleep on the couch. She must have been exhausted when she finally fell asleep. I wondered if she was not used to doing all the physical activity she had done yesterday, but it was not my place to ask. Not yet.

Instead, I simply walked quietly through the living room and into the kitchen. She'd probably wake up to the smell of food. I didn't want to wake her up yet, but my stomach was growling. So, instead of immediately pulling out a pan, I made sure that I had the ingredients for some breakfast burritos.

Tortillas, eggs, hashbrowns, sausage, cheese, and some vegetables. I liked mushrooms, bell peppers, and a good crunchy hashbrown in my breakfast tortillas, but I suddenly realized that I had no idea what she liked. I made a mental note to ask her—and to pay more attention. She'd noticed what I'd eaten for nearly every meal since she'd moved in, and I hadn't particularly noticed anything she'd made.

The smell of eggs would probably wake her up. If she wanted eggs cooked in another manner, I could make that happen.

I pulled out a pan to start frying up things and preheated the oven for the hashbrowns. Then, I buttered up the pan for my eggs. Just a little bit of butter for taste with a bit of salt and pepper. I'd add the hot sauce after I had assembled my burrito just in case Jade didn't want any.

Chapter Twenty

Twenty: Jade

The next morning, I woke up to the smell of breakfast. I slowly rubbed my eyes, sitting up. Something slid off my shoulder, and I then realized that there was a blanket around me. When had I gotten the blanket? I didn't remember waking up in the middle of the night to get one.

I shook my head, rose, and walked into the kitchen. There were tortillas sitting on the counter, and the smells of eggs, hashbrowns, mushrooms, and other vegetables meant that Jesse was probably making some kind of breakfast burrito. It smelled good. I wondered, briefly, if he would be willing to share with me.

"Go ahead and take a seat," Jesse said. "Hungry?"

"Very." I took a seat at the counter, not sure what else to do.

As the cobwebs of sleep started clearing in my brain, I suddenly realized he had probably come home and found me asleep on the couch in the living room. I was renting the entire upstairs and had fallen asleep in the living room. How embarrassing. However, it didn't seem to bother Jesse one bit. He didn't even mention it.

Maybe he had fallen asleep on that couch before and knew that sometimes, it was less about what was comfiest and more about what was close by because you were so exhausted.

"Did you have a good evening?" I decided it was time to try and make some conversation.

Based on previous interactions, I didn't really expect this one to go anywhere. To my surprise, Jesse turned to face me.

"It was as good as it could be, I suppose," he said. "Somewhat emotional."

I pursed my lips. I hadn't meant to make him feel emotional last night. However, I supposed if he was getting emotional, it was a good place to start. His walls were coming down... and that was honestly the last thing I had ever expected.

"I'm sorry if I said something upsetting," I said softly. "That was not my intention at all last night." I pursed my lips.

I wasn't sure what else to say. Or what I could say. It wasn't like I could convince Jesse that I hadn't meant to pry. I surely hadn't, but it kind of looked that way no matter what I said.

"Actually, it was something you said that made me realize perhaps I've been too harsh with you," Jesse admitted. "I think it's time you learned where I have been going when I don't have a shift at the fire house or plans here."

I raised an eyebrow. It seemed that I had been able to get through to him after all. It wasn't at all what I thought we'd be doing this morning. However, after the breakfast burritos had been finished on the pan, he handed me a plate with two. I smiled a little. At least he was learning. That was good.

I remained at the counter. He took a seat next to me.

"All right. So where do you go?" I asked. "It's clearly somewhere important to you."

"I go to the Chandler Ranch. My routine is a shift at the fire station, and if I don't have anything else to do here, I go to the ranch. Sometimes, this means I'm only in the house for like twenty-four hours before I go," he said. "I didn't anticipate that it would be hard for someone to grasp that I had a lot of things on my plate without hearing of the details."

"What's the Chandler Ranch?" I asked.

I had not heard of this place before, but it sounded quite important to him. I didn't understand why he hadn't told me before. This didn't really feel like a deep, dark secret, but I guessed that maybe I'd underestimated just how closed-off Jesse was used to being. If this felt significant to him, I could accept that and appreciate it.

"I grew up on the ranch. That might be part of why I'm not a fan of the city," he said, a soft blush on his cheeks. "Anyway, I'm sorry for hiding where I was going. I've only just now realized that you were probably asking what my schedule was like out of concern or worry when I would just disappear before you even got up."

"How far away is the ranch?" I pursed my lips before taking a bite of the breakfast burrito on my plate.

"It's about two hours away. So, I'm usually gone for a couple of days at a time when I go," he replied.

I nodded slowly. It sounded as though this ranch was a tie to his family, but that could have meant a variety of things. He could have been part of the family that owned it, or part of one of the families that worked on it. There was really no way to tell, and I didn't want to ask that. It felt too personal right now.

He had only just started to open up to me. What kind of person would I be if I asked that question now?

"Why mention the ranch now?" I pursed my lips.

It simply seemed to be the right time," he said. "I know it's not nearly enough to make up for the way I've treated you, but I was hoping we might be able to start with a clean slate from here?"

"And when you can no longer fight fires with that being such an extremely physical job, is that what you plan to do? Work at the ranch?" I asked.

"Pretty much. They have plenty of things I could do that won't necessarily include being physically involved with the animals or the hard physical work."

I nodded, seeing Jesse in a whole new light.

Chapter Twenty-One

Twenty-One: Jesse

I watched, eating my breakfast, as Jade processed my plans. What I hadn't mentioned to her yet was that one of the main reasons I planned to return to the ranch when I could no longer fight fires was because I knew my parents would always have a place for me there. But that didn't seem important to tell her right now. Besides, Jade was somewhat right. When it was time for me to stop fighting the fires, I would probably be too physically done to be on the ranch in the capacity I was in right now.

Especially if she worried that I would hurt myself.

That thought hit me across the back of the head so hard that I almost stopped eating. Almost. Jade was still eating her breakfast burritos in silence, and I managed to avoid swallowing anything wrong. I was always so worried about other people that I'd never really stopped to consider that someone besides my parents might worry about me.

And, although I at least considered the opinions of my parents, I mostly lived to the beat of my own drum.

Knowing that I'd be willing to compromise for someone like Jade made me wonder if there was more to this relationship we were creating than first met the eyes. I hadn't thought I would find a woman while working so much, but it seemed that she had found the perfect way to nestle into my life and break down my walls.

"I think it's really amazing you have such an honest work ethic," she finally said. "Well, if you're going to be away from home that much, would it be too much to ask that you let me know when you've arrived safely at the ranch or even when you've arrived safely at home?"

"Why would I do that?" I furrowed my eyebrows.

It was an odd request, but that might partially be because I hadn't been part of a relationship where it was expected before.

"I've had other friends do that for me," she explained. "We'll text when we get home safely after meeting up so that the other doesn't have to worry about safety." She shrugged. "I feel that, as you are my landlord and my roommate, I do deserve to know that you're safe. I'd hate to learn from someone else that I was homeless."

I couldn't help but give a soft chuckle at that. She had a point. She deserved to know that I was safe if only to give her peace of mind.

"I think I can do that, then, if that's the reasoning behind the request," I said. "It may take me a while to get used to it."

"As long as you tell me that you've arrived safely at some point," she clarified. "We've both got a life outside of what we do when we're home together. I understand that."

"It probably won't have to be done until after the fundraiser, if I'm honest," I said. "Unless it counts for my shifts at the firehouse, too."

"Since you leave so early in the morning, it'd be nice to know that you got there safely," she said. "I've got my phone set up so that it won't ring at night, so you won't be disturbing my sleep by texting me that you've arrived home safely. Or there."

I nodded slowly. That was also a good thing to know. Being in the house with Jade was a good thing, but I had plenty of other things to do today.

"Well, I was asked to come in today, but if I'm going to make it on time for the shift change that I was given, I have to leave in the next half hour," I said. "I just thought that it would be a good idea to share some answers that you've been digging for while we had breakfast."

"I appreciate that," she said. "Maria and I are opening our store today at ten, so I've got to get ready to leave too. Thanks for sharing, and I hope you drive safely to the fire station. The rain last night may have made the roads slick."

I smiled a little. It was good to know that she cared for me. Something in me warmed at the thought—I wasn't used to that feeling, but it was nice.

I shook my head and reminded myself it was probably just because she was a good person who always tried to be nice to people.

With that, I put my dishes in the sink and went to get ready for my shift. I didn't have too much to get ready, but I did throw together a small bag of extra clothing. There was never any way to predict what would happen while on shift. While there was a washer and a drier at the station, it didn't work all that well. I preferred to do my laundry at home, so I just took extra changes of clothes. .

There was only so much our equipment could do to keep the smell from permeating our skin and our clothing.

After I was all packed up, I hefted the bag up onto my shoulders and then went out to the living room. Jade was gone. She had probably gone upstairs. I took my bag out to the truck and then noticed that she was on the phone with someone in the window seat in the room that looked over the driveway. I waved at her as I got in the truck to leave.

To my surprise, she waved back with a soft smile.

I smiled and started the truck. With that, I drove carefully to the fire station. It was a road I'd driven hundreds of time, but something today felt different. I realized that I was wondering what Jade would want to do when my shift was done since I wasn't planning to go to the ranch again until after the fundraiser was over.

I kind of liked thinking about that, and I smiled as I rolled down my window.

Chapter Twenty-Two

Twenty-Two: Jade

Once I was off the phone with Maria, I realized that there was a text from Jesse. He'd made it safely. I was glad to know that he was going to be taking my feelings into consideration when he was trying to make plans now. At least, just enough to let me know that he had arrived safely – no matter where it was or what his plans were.

Today, *my* plans were relatively simple. We were opening the store. Officially.

Ordinarily, this day would have probably gotten a bit more fanfare, but Maria had had something pop up at the last minute, so she couldn't be there for our grand opening. It was a bummer, but she had given me full permission to go on without her. Our biggest boost for publicity would happen at the fundraiser, so a "soft" opening seemed totally acceptable.

I needed to get going. I wanted to get to the store no later than nine this morning to open promptly at ten.

I had made a ton of jewelry over the last couple of days that had nothing to do with the fundraiser but that I could display at the store. We'd had some more jewelry displays come in before the store opened, and I wanted to have some extra inventory in the back of the store to allow people to keep browsing a full inventory on the floor.

Maria had put *plenty* of purses in the back already. She'd already had an overflow at home. And this wasn't even half of it if I remembered correctly. She'd been sewing purses like this for a long time and just hadn't had anywhere to store them or sell them.

I took a deep breath as I carried things out to the car. With Jesse gone, it was so quiet in the house. I wondered if I would find his noise endearing now that we were getting along. I already kind of missed his voice.

I shook those thoughts away. Once I packed all the extra jewelry safely in the back of my car, I drove to the store. Upon arriving, I was a little glad to learn I had arrived a half hour earlier than I even meant to. That would give me plenty of time to set up the new jewelry displays and make sure all the posters were up properly for our fundraiser. We'd be closing the store for that, but that was only because we were going to be at the expo center and hadn't yet hired enough employees to be able to run both at once.

I hoped that by next year, we could keep the store running *and* have a fundraiser stall going at the expo center.

That was also a rather ambitious thought. We hadn't even officially opened yet!

I took the time to put up the rest of the jewelry displays. I even managed to put up a few displays that mounted on the wall. I was pretty impressed with how great they looked, and I started filling them with jewelry I had brought from home.

Once I was done with the new displays, I had a single jewelry box still filled out of the four large plastic ones I had brought with me. Thankfully, I had also anticipated this. I'd brought a bunch of beading supplies and some of the fundraiser colors to make sure that I could keep busy while people browsed.

Ten o'clock in the morning finally came around, and I had managed to make a few bracelets in the meantime. The earrings I would be making at home. Always. The felt work was too complicated to put down and restart multiple times, in my opinion. There were probably plenty of people who could do it while talking to others and taking breaks without getting lost. I simply hadn't gotten there yet.

"Welcome!" I smiled as I saw the first customer come through the door. "Come on in. Grand opening today."

He smiled.

"Have anything that says, 'I want to be your boyfriend'?" he asked.

I pursed my lips. That was an odd request, but I was sure that if he just looked around, he would find something.

"That entirely depends on what she likes. Don't be shy," I said as I motioned around to the jewelry and the other artsy items on sale. "Have a look. I'm sure that if you can't find the perfect piece of jewelry, there might be something else that she'd like! We have some beautiful purses as well."

He nodded slowly and then started to look around. I didn't have time to start up another beading project because more customers were coming in. I was soon ringing people up and making sure the tags matched the prices I was putting into the system. Maria had done her own pricing, and they looked reasonable for the amount of time and material I knew went into what she made.

The jewelry appeared to be a little more of an eyecatcher for most, but with some sticker shock. I had based my prices off what the most popular pieces were in my online store, adjusted for the fact that they were not paying for shipping. I wondered if I hadn't adjusted the prices enough, but the jewelry was still coming off the walls and displays faster than I could put it out.

We needed to have more than two employees if we were going to run this store properly, in my opinion.

Around noon, I finally got a bit of a break. Instead of sitting down to bead, I decided that it would be better to eat the sandwich I had brought in for my lunch. I wasn't sure when I'd get another break, and there was no telling if this pattern would hold.

About half-way through my sandwich, the bell over the door rang. I looked up to see a man walking in.

"You should give up the lease for this building," he said, a set frown on his face as he spoke. "It's big city folk like you that have *ruined* our little town!"

"May I help you sir?" I asked, suddenly very aware of how alone I was in the store.

I didn't want to indulge the crazy person, but something told me that I'd have to at least hear him out to get him out of the shop.

"Give up this lease! Quit this place!"

And he stopped making sense to me after that, talking about a business that should have succeeded, but people were too stupid to see the beauty in what had been happening here before we arrived. I grabbed my cell phone.

"Sir, I'm going to have to ask you to step outside."

He kept talking, beginning to gesticulate wildly in the air, stabbing a pointed finger at the purses, curtains, and jewelry.

"Sir," I said again more loudly. "Please leave, or I'll call the police."

Even with my voice raised, I tried to sound as calm and authoritative as possible. He narrowed his eyes at me, but I decided to go ahead and dial the line anyway. This startled him out of the shop.

Instead of hanging up to call the non-emergency line, I gave a description of the guy to the first responders and apologized for the last-second bump to a non-emergency, but I didn't want to have cops coming to the shop if I could help it.

"Now, just be careful. Sometimes, these people are just off their meds," the first responder said. "And if they're willing to leave when you threaten to call the cops, maybe they've realized that they need to step back and calm down."

"He didn't leave until I dialed," I admitted.

"Either way, you have a record of the incident, and I hope that at least makes you feel better," he said. "Have a good day, ma'am."

"Thank you. You too."

I let him hang up on my call, taking a deep breath.

The rest of the day was a whirl because business picked up quickly around one. Thankfully, I'd been able to put out some new stock, eat my sandwich, and take a few minutes to take a deep breath before the next customers came in. It would have been a thousand times easier if Maria had been able to make it, but I understood that it didn't always happen the way we wanted it to.

At five p.m., I shut the front door and flipped the sign to read 'closed.' It'd take me a half hour or so to get everything all figured out as far as the cleaning went, but that wouldn't be the worst thing in the world.

"Well, one day down. A million more to go, hopefully," I said as I went to the back for a broom.

The cleaning went well enough. I turned on some music on my phone so that it didn't feel like I was alone in the store. That was a creepy feeling that I didn't want to worry about.

By the time I was done, I was ready to go. My stomach was growling, and for a good day's work, I had decided to pick up a pizza on the way home. I locked the front door so that I could go out the back, and then, headed towards the back door.

And it was then that I smelled it.

Something burning. I hurried to grab the fire extinguisher and then found myself in the back room, where a fire had broken out among the purses. I tried to put it out, but the fire was too strong. Unnaturally strong. As if someone had used an accelerant to make sure the fire would spread faster than I could put it out.

How did this start?

I began coughing as the smoke started getting thicker in the air. I tried to get to the back door. I reached it only to find that it had been blocked by something. It opened outward, but I couldn't push it open for the life of me. By now, the fire had spread to cut me off from the front of the store.

With a pounding heart, I realized I was trapped.

I checked my pocket and found my phone.

My fingers fumbled a little as panic set in, but I was able to dial 911.

"911. What's your emergency?"

"Fire... send firefighters..." I managed to cough this out, and started to say the address as I lowered myself to my knees. "I'm stuck. The door is blocked"

"We'll have EMS and fire there right away. What's your name?"

"Jade. Jade Santana."

"All right, Miss Santana. Can you get to a window?"

I attempted to respond, but the panic, the smoke, and the adrenaline conspired against me. There weren't any windows in the back room, and the lack of ventilation was concentrating the smoke. My eyes started to feel heavier, and the phone fell out of my hands. All I could do was protect my head as I fell all the way to the ground, hoping that this would not be the end.

Chapter Twenty-Three

Twenty-Three: Jesse

The first day of a shift was usually uneventful. Today, that was incredibly not the case. As we were winding down for the evening, a call came in for EMS and fire. As we hurried to the trucks, the dispatcher read out the address. I realized I recognized it.

Jade's shop. That was Jade's shop. I sprinted to the fire truck and climbed into the driver's seat.

"I know how to get there. I'll drive," I called to the rest of the men. "EMS has been called to the scene. Someone's inside that building. *Let's go!*"

I flipped the sirens on, and the men ran through their prep. As soon as the men on my truck were ready, I was racing through the streets. All I could hear were the sirens and the screeching of my tires as I made tight turns, thanks to some people who didn't want to clear the way.

Eventually, we were able to make it through the traffic jam and get to the store. From the front of the building, it didn't look so bad which made me think it might have been a small fire, but when we got close, you could see black smoke billowing out from the back room. But I couldn't see Jade.

On the way, we'd gotten briefed on the 911 call. They said a woman had called the fire in, but hadn't been able to finish the call. Was it Jade? Had she made it out?

The first responder on the phone line couldn't get anything out of her but could hear her wheezing. I started gearing up and went around to the back. My heart plummeted when I saw Jade's car, but what I saw next was worse.

Someone had dragged a full wooden dresser up to the back of the building and jammed it into the back door. And there were no other outlets from the back room except through the front.

"Break the front door down! That's our quickest way in!" I called around to the front. "Hurry! We've got a person in here."

I hurried back around front to see everyone fussing with the hoses. This was something I'd have to do myself. I put my mask on and grabbed an axe. As much work as Jade had put into this place, the door had to go.

Moving through protocol with perfected ease, I first checked to see if it was locked. It was. So, down the door went by breaking the locked knob off. As I stepped in, I noticed the fire spreading to the front room. Jade must have been getting ready to leave through the back door when it started, which is why she hadn't been able to get out.

I made it into the back room, and one of the firemen used a hose to help keep a path clear for me to bring Jade out. I found her collapsed on the floor, surrounded by some of the hottest flames but not yet engulfed by them. Her phone was collateral damage at this point, but that could be easily replaced.

A quick glance told me that she needed immediate medical attention. She had burns on her abdomen and on her arm, and I could only imagine how much smoke she'd inhaled. I gently picked her up, holding her close.

The flames were beginning to burn hotter, which made me wonder what kind of fire this was. Or it was just because the fire didn't have anywhere else to go. Thankfully, the hose running in the front room was enough to cool the pathway to prevent another flare-up.

As I hurried Jade out, I heard the ever-recognizable sirens of an ambulance.

"She's still breathing, but barely," I told the first EMS responder who hopped out of the ambulance. "She was in there when the fire started."

"Put her on the stretcher," the paramedic told me.

I put her down gently, and let the professionals handle what they could. It didn't surprise me at all to hear that they were going to end up taking her to the hospital.

"All right! Let's get this fire out. Get me a hose!" I called to my men.

One of them brought me a hose. I put my helmet and oxygen mask back on and went back inside. I'd be able to do more from the inside. With the pressure of the fire hose, I was able to calm the flames enough to let others in from the back to help after they were able to move the dresser. Once the fire was out, it was quite evident that Jade had a singed, soaked shop.

"Who would do this to this shop?" one of my men asked as we started putting the equipment away after making sure the fire wouldn't flare up again. "This shop's had a run of bad luck... and this woman just started."

"It was her grand opening," I replied. "But for now, I think we're safe. If there's a flare-up, we know what to do. Let's get back to the station."

I took one last walk through the shop. Though there was a lot of water pooling on the floor, and I was almost sure the purses that Maria had made that were here were destroyed with the amount of water we had needed to use, I hoped they had insurance. This was clearly not negligence. There wasn't a candle or a lighter anywhere near here. The most I hoped to find was ash, which might have once been a match.

But there was a sweet smell in the air. Like someone had used lighter fluid to get this going.

I shook my head. The theories could wait until I knew for sure that Jade was going to be alright. Someone would have to call Maria, and I didn't have her number. Jade's cell phone was useless right now, and it absolutely needed to be dried out.

One of the other men drove the truck back to the fire station upon seeing the state I was in.

"You're not usually so quiet after a fire, Jesse," he said. "What's got you going?"

"I don't think that was an accidental fire or an electrical fire," I replied. "I think someone set it intentionally. I don't think it was the shop owner, either. She called 911 and almost died. Who does that if they've put their own shop on fire while they're *inside* it?"

"Could have been an attempt at insurance fraud, but she looked so sweet. I doubt she would have been trying that," my friend said. "It's a real piece of work. We'll just have to do some testing. I know one of the other men got air samples. I think he said he smelled something sweet. Sent it off to the forensics lab for testing."

I nodded. That was good. Meant I wasn't the only one smelling the accelerant. If that was the case, then we had a better case for arson to present to everyone.

Chapter Twenty-Four

Twenty-Four: Jade

I groaned heavily as I tried to open my eyes. The last thing I remembered was passing out in my shop with a fire burning around me. Though I had a feeling that I had been in Jesse's arms. But now, I didn't smell the tell-tale signs of purses burning or the smell of the wood heating up underneath my feet. I smelled lemon and antiseptic spray or soap or something like that.

When my eyes finally opened, I was greeted by a bright light overhead. I blinked, my first instinct to look away. This is when I finally noticed that there was a sensation of heat all across my right arm and my abdomen. Instead of looking right at the light as I opened my eyes, I looked down at my body. My right arm was in gauze bandages, as was my midriff. Peeking out from under the bandages, I could see the irritated tell-tale red of a burn.

A nurse walked in.

This is when I realized I had to be in the hospital. I didn't remember calling 911 for help, but I must have. I was the only one in the shop. Our fire alarms worked, but I couldn't remember if they had gone off or not.

"Oh, good. You're awake. The doctors said you might take a day or two to wake up," the nurse said as she walked over. "I'm Felicity. I'll be your nurse this morning."

I managed a smile, then realized my throat was sore, scratchy, dry. I motioned for a cup.

"I can get you some water." Felicity smiled. "Your throat might feel a little dry and scratchy for the next couple of days. You took in quite a bit of smoke when you passed out. Thank goodness you were able to call 911. Could have been a lot worse if you hadn't." She brought a small paper cup of water over from the sink. "Here. Careful. Use your left hand. Your right hand might sting a little if you do too much too soon."

I nodded. I followed her instructions. She took some vital signs, checked on my burns, and then left to go get one of the doctors. I settled in to be alone for a while because this was a big hospital, but I was not alone for long.

"Oh, thank goodness! You're awake," Maria's voice entered the room. "I came by yesterday to see how you were doing and was so worried. Thank goodness Jesse and his team responded to that fire."

"Jesse?" My voice came out scratchy and hoarse.

I found it really hurt to talk right now. I took another sip of water.

"Jesse found my number and told me about the fire and that you were in the hospital. They're investigating what happened," Maria said as she sat down.

"Actually, I think we have a pretty good case for arson."

I looked behind Maria to see Jesse walking in. He carried a small stuffed bear that said "get well soon" on a heart the little bear held in its arms. He set it on the table in front of my bed.

"Thank you."

I managed a smile. Though my voice was hoarse, I wanted him to know how much I appreciated the job he had done when he had come to see what had happened. I hadn't expected him to show up, but seeing him made my stomach do a little flip. He looked relieved that I was awake, and I couldn't help but notice how kind his face looked as he took in my bandages.

"It's my job, Jade," Jesse replied. "Your store is alright. A little waterlogged from having to put out the fire, but fine. You're going to need a new doorknob on the front door, though. We had to break it to get in because there wasn't time to move the dresser that was placed in front of the back door. Someone set that fire on purpose."

"Oh, my..." Maria's face went pale.

"Don't worry. We left it secure. But yeah," Jessie finished, "ultimately you'll need a new door. Sorry about that."

I would have been lying to myself if I tried to say that I was so distracted by the fact that he'd saved my life that I didn't care about the door at all. What had we done to deserve that kind of treatment? Who would have done that to a store only trying to bring some joy into the world?

"Maria, why don't you go find us some food? I'm sure Jade is starving."

"I can do that. Something easy to chew, easy to swallow for Jade, I'm sure, would be good. Right?" Maria looked at me.

I nodded. That sounded like a good idea. I mimed licking an ice cream cone. Maria laughed.

"I'll see what kind of popsicles or ice cream I can find you. It may be a hot minute before I return." With that, Maria left the room, glancing suggestively from me to Jesse behind his back before she closed the door.

This left me alone with Jesse. He appeared to have come right from the fire station because I could still smell hints of smoke on him. At least he wasn't fresh from a fire. I don't know if I could have handled smelling a ton of smoke right now. The little bit I could smell was making me a little queasy.

"I know I probably smell a little like smoke," he said as if he could read my mind. "But I've had to answer two fire calls today. It doesn't wash out easily," he said. "I had to come talk to you. To see that you were all right. Finding you passed out on the floor of the shop... I don't ever want to see you in a position like that again."

I nodded. I never wanted to be in that position again. It had been terrible, not knowing what to do. I remembered my brain fuzzing over as panic set in, despite doing my best to follow the prompts given to me by the operator on the phone.

"I'm so relieved we got to you in time," he said with so much sincerity in his voice that it made me blush. "I must admit that there is... there is another reason I came to see you."

I looked at him curiously.

"Working with you for the fundraiser gave me a chance to get to know you, and then the fire – and — I feel close to you after all of this. Would you... would you be willing to give me a second chance? I know I've done little to deserve it, but I would like to start over." He couldn't meet my eyes, no matter what he tried to do while he spoke.

It was touching. This event had clearly sparked some remorse. I couldn't tell what had caused the change, but I wondered if it had anything to do with the fact that I had been found on the floor of the shop, with nasty burns. Despite doing the right thing. Like his friend all those years ago.

I nodded slowly. He wouldn't meet my eyes, but I was sure he was aware of my nodding.

A small smile spread across his face.

"I'm glad to hear it," he said, finally looking up, his piecing eyes shining into mine.

Chapter Twenty-Five

Twenty-Five: Jesse

A warm, fuzzy feeling spread through my chest seeing Jade nod that she was willing to give me a second chance. The smile that spread with it wasn't something I had meant to show Jade, but perhaps that was a good thing. That she was able to see it. She deserved to know that there was more to me than just the grumpy man she had gotten to know over the past few weeks.

"Well, I should be going. I have a shift to get back to." I stood up, a bit sad to leave her. I'd have gladly spent the whole day sitting in the hospital with her.

She nodded and put a hand on mine – as if to tell me that she understood. I was only glad that she wasn't trying to strain her voice for me. She didn't need to end up in more pain because she was trying to tell me that it was all okay. Or would be soon.

Before I could leave the room, Maria returned. She had found food, all right – but it wasn't just for her and Jade. There was a third plate. Had she gotten a plate for me too, despite knowing that I was probably going to have to leave?

"I hope you're not leaving just yet, Mr. Delaney," Maria said as she helped Jade get situated on the bed so that she could eat her ice cream.

"You deserve a little more of a break than just coming to check on Jade. I think you can spare five minutes for your mental health."

I looked to Jade, who looked at Maria a moment longer before nodding in my direction. If Jade agreed, then I supposed the only thing to do was to stay as asked. I sat back down.

"Let me check with the chief," I said. "I'd hate to give you both false hope."

Jade nodded. Maria was too busy opening the ice cream to bother with much more than a soft nod in my direction.

I pulled my phone out of my pocket, only to find that the chief had texted me while I had been talking to Jade. He simply wanted me to know that they could spare me all day if I felt I needed to be gone that long. They understood that this was someone I had been close to, and they wanted me to be sure that I would be able to perform my job to the best of my ability. If I needed to take a bit of time off to make sure she was okay, he understood and supported that.

I appreciated that.

"It seems I'm all clear for today," I told them. "The chief says I can take the day if I need it. They're some pretty understanding guys that I work with. I'm not entirely shocked he's having me take a day."

"That's good to hear," Maria said.

Jade didn't add much to the conversation we had after other than the occasional head shake or nod, but I didn't mind. She was feeling better and was awake. It reminded me that I had brought something for Jade. With that, I went back out to my car to get it.

However, on my way back in with the beading kit, I passed the large main desk. Then, it hit me. Jade and Maria were self-employed and may not have had health insurance. Or if they did, it may not have covered something like what happened to Jade. I knew unexpected hospital stays could quickly add up. Instead of leaving Jade to drown in debt, I decided that the least that I could do was pay her hospital bills. So, I stopped by the main desk.

"How can I help you today?"

"I'm here to put in a billing address and card for Jade Santana's bills," I said. "Am I allowed to do that?"

"Yes." She began typing, I assumed to pull up Jade's forms.

"I wish to anonymously pay her bills for her. I don't think she's got any health insurance, and I hate to see dreams crushed by the debt of an unforeseen accident," I said. "But please don't tell her it was me."

The woman at the desk nodded slowly and allowed me to go ahead and pay off what she already had racked up – and allowed me to put in an address for a bill at a later date. I put in the address of the ranch. I didn't want her to find out what I was doing, at least, not accidentally. I'd tell her. Eventually.

I just wasn't sure how comfortable she'd be with it.

When I returned to the right floor and got closer to her room, I caught bits of the conversation she was having with Maria. Well, I caught what *Maria* was saying. Jade may have been typing it out on a phone or writing out on paper what she wanted to say. It sounded as though they were discussing bills.

"Hi."

I did the courteous thing and let them know I was coming in by speaking up as I walked in.

"Do you happen to know if this hospital does payment plans?" Maria looked at me. "Jade's worried about the bill. We don't have health insurance yet, and this is going to cream our savings if we're not careful about how it is done."

I paused for an awkwardly long time, trying to figure out what to say. Eventually, I spoke. "It's already been taken care of," I said. "You have nothing to worry about, Jade." I knew I'd have to tell her the truth sooner or later. I guess the universe had decided I should tell her now.

"How?"

Jade's voice was still hoarse, but not nearly as hoarse as earlier. Her throat was probably feeling a little better if she managed to say a single word to me. I was glad to hear her voice getting better, but still didn't think it was a good idea for her to be speaking much yet.

"The Ranch is kind to people who work there," I replied simply. "But I think the better question is, are you going to be able to do anything about the fundraiser? Oh, and I brought this for you." I hoped drawing her attention back to the fundraiser and her beading would keep her from asking more questions about her bills.

I put the beading kit on the table, and her face lit up. She immediately started to work on a new pair of earrings, and I could tell that the work of beading was relaxing her. I smiled a little. I loved watching her work.

***

It didn't end up mattering what happened at the fundraiser, because Jade was able to make it. She had to sit in a chair all day and had to be under an umbrella to shade her injuries, but she made it.

"If you need anything at all from me, let me know," I said as we finished setting up the small booth they had been able to put together. "I'm more than willing to run errands or run around looking for someone or something for you two. Especially since half of you are out of commission as far as running around goes." I didn't want to come across as clingy, but I really wanted to make sure Jade was okay. This would be a long day for her after such significant injuries.

"Thank you, Jesse," Jade said. "I think we'll be all right, but if my throat acts up, I'm sending you to get ice cream." She grinned, and it might have been my imagination, but I think the sun got a little brighter.

"A vanilla sundae with whipped cream and a cherry. I know," I said with a soft smile. "Now, is that all you need of me for now? Setting up the tables?"

"If you could help me set up the purses, I'd definitely appreciate it," Maria said.

I did exactly that, and the fundraiser started shortly after we had the booth all set up. Jade sat behind the table of jewelry, which was sparkling in the light that had begun to come through the cracks in the tarp and the umbrella. It was stunning. It showed exactly how beautiful her jewelry could be for photography or for any event someone could think of. I thought it was a great way to show off how her jewelry could be used.

I sat to the side, letting Maria and Jade interact with the customers. The fundraiser itself wasn't the most exciting thing in the world for me. But I could tell that others were having fun. There were food stands, lemonade stands, and even some entertainers who had decided that they could get in on the fun. One of them was a fire breather, and that had always drawn a crowd from what I understood. I was just glad to see that everyone was having fun.

As people came by and noticed the sparkling jewelry, Jade's display dwindled. No one could walk away from the booth without getting *something* from her.

By the end of the day, all Jade had to take down were her displays. Maria had sold all but two of the purses they had brought – including the ones in the cars that I had been sent to get when the stock in the booth ran low.

Jade also ended up selling out of her entire inventory online, so the fundraiser had gone rather well for our little booth. As I walked with Jade and Maria back to the truck, Jade wore an absolutely glowing smile. As did Maria.

"That was so much fun!" Maria said. "I want to do this again next year. I think if we're careful and reserve stock all year long, we could do even better and raise even more money for you guys. This year was kind of haphazard because we just got started in the shop."

"I'm somewhat shocked you sold out. We're not used to someone selling out like that," I admitted. "From what I've heard from the chief, no one sells out. Not like this. A few might run out of a particular product, but no one legitimately sells out their entire inventory on the day of the fundraiser."

"It wasn't our entire inventory," Jade corrected him. "We still have a fully-stocked shop to run! But yes, we did sell out all of our inventory that we'd allotted for the fundraiser." She did a little happy dance through the parking lot.

"Well, still," I said. "Did you want to get a ride home with me or were you ladies going to swing by your store?"

"I don't need to go to the store," Maria said, waving her hand. "I'm planning on going straight home, putting my feet up, and celebrating with a glass of wine. We did well today."

I helped Jade up into the truck, which we had decided would be the only vehicle we'd use today because it had more space for inventory if we needed it at the end of the day. With that, we all headed home.

As I drove, Jade fell fast asleep in the seat beside me. I didn't mind it. She had had a long week, and to go do this after what had happened at the store was a testament of her strength to me.

As we drove down the road, I figured she just might be the most wonderful person I'd ever met.

Chapter Twenty-Six

Twenty-Six: Jade

The next three months were amazing. The store flourished but more importantly, Jesse and I flourished. I was falling head over heels in love with this guy. He was tender and considerate, made me laugh, and would hold me so affectionately in his arms. When I told him about my feelings for him, he whispered in my ear that he loved me too.

Then, one weekend, he decided it was time for me to see the ranch and meet his family. We enjoyed a beautiful drive, although I drifted in and out of sleep a couple of times. I'd stayed up late the night before, beading as always.

Maria's and my store was thriving. We'd fixed everything up after the fire, and business was booming. We sold at least one thing every day (even on the slow ones!) and most weekends we burned through our inventory like crazy.

Still a ways out from the ranch, Jesse woke me when he started pointing out some of the property of the ranch owners. It was amazing. As far as the eye could see.

When we arrived at the ranch, I was stunned. This had to be the most spectacular log cabin I had ever seen. It was a mansion! A big veranda, huge wooden double doors serving as the main entrance, and gigantic windows all around.

Jesse excused himself for a moment and jogged over to one of the workers coming out of one of the smaller buildings on the property. He returned within a minute. We entered the house through the double doors.

Inside was even more breath-taking — vaulted ceilings, fireplaces, spacious rooms.

"Seeing your mouth wide open reminds me that I'm hungry," Jesse mused. "Let me see what I can find in the kitchen. Make yourself comfortable."

I wasn't sure how he expected me to just chill on a couch when there was so much to look at! I wandered to a large window to take in the view. All that kept going through my mind was "this is absolutely amazing."

After what seemed like only a few minutes, Jesse called to me from the dining room. I could see him from where I stood with all the open rooms. He set a pizza down at the table. I joined him.

Here we were, sitting in the dining room of the Chandler Ranch. I had to admit that I was flummoxed with how to proceed. We'd started dating, yes, but he hadn't told me the ranch was nearly this beautiful. Or nearly this elegant and huge!

"Here we are. One pizza from the best place around," Jesse said, grinning. "Enjoy."

"Thank you, Jesse," I said with a smile.

As we set to eating the pizza, Jesse said, "I think you drifted off to sleep a couple of times on the way here."

"Yeah... I do that sometimes on long road trips," I admitted sheepishly before taking a bite of pizza. "Store's doing so well now, but I still lose track of time when I'm beading at night. The fire station fundraiser boosted our sales enough that we have the income stream to hire more people. Did I tell you we found someone to be our new full-time cashier? And someone who can help make jewelry?"

"That's wonderful," Jesse said as he put a slice of pizza on his plate. "What's Maria doing while you're here?"

"Maria is working on designing our holiday collections now," I replied. "She has an eye for the design element of the job, and between that and the purses, she's pretty busy most of the time."

"Well, as long as you two are happy with the way things have turned out, then I say it's a win," Jesse continued. "I'm glad to see that the store can function a few days without you so long as the inventory is up to speed."

"Or we've got the beading people in the shop making more instead of with our online sales," I admitted. "Either way, it's going to be great."

Jesse smiled.

"I'm glad to hear that you're able to take these new steps with the shop." He took my hand and squeezed it gently before letting go so that we could eat.

And eat we did in comfortable silence. After we had learned how to best communicate with each other, the silences had stopped feeling so awkward. Now, it was like we didn't need to say anything to each other. I appreciated this. There weren't many people in the world with whom I felt comfortable with prolonged silence. For Jesse to be one of them was a good thing, considering we lived together.

My phone rang as I was swallowing the last bites of my pizza.

"You should get that. I'll go put the extra pizza away," Jesse said as he stood up.

I answered the phone.

"Is this Jade Santana speaking?"

"This is she. How may I help you?" I had forgotten to look at the caller ID, but I suspected that this was important from the way the person on the phone was speaking.

"My name is Detective Cordova with the Lantana police," the voice said. "I'm calling about the arson at your artisanal shop."

"Oh!" I had almost completely forgotten about the investigation going on.

The fire station was almost sure that it was arson, and they had been working with the local police to figure it out. Whatever had happened, I was just glad that things were going to be resolved properly.

"Do you have news for me?" I continued, hoping that there would be a development.

The case had been lying stagnant for a while, but not for a lack of trying on the detectives' part. Even Jesse had been doing some investigation as a firefighter. But nothing had come up. Yet. I hoped that there was finally news. Even if it was just an update of what had caused the fire or how it had spread so quickly.

"I do," Detective Cordova started. "We've caught the arsonist."

I gasped in surprise. This was such good news!

"It seems the previous owner of the building had a business that failed there. He was selling taxidermy turkeys, which as you can imagine, did not sell well. He apparently decided that if his business failed in that building, then no business in that building would succeed. You just happened to be in the wrong place at the wrong time."

"Thank you for the information, Detective," I said. "He has been arrested, yes? He's not going to be a problem anymore for the community?"

"He won't be a problem any longer," the detective confirmed. "We just thought that you would be interested in hearing this news, considering what happened to you because of his actions."

"Thank you."

I smiled widely as I hung up the phone. Jesse had appeared in the doorway, and he raised his eyebrows in question.

"Was that news about the arsonist? He's been caught, then, from that conversation you just had on the phone?" He walked over to meet me at the table.

I nodded.

"Caught and arrested," I replied. "Thank goodness. Now, we just have to wait for him to be sentenced."

"You should sue him for the damages and lost wages as well," Jesse said, sitting down. "I know a great lawyer who could take the case for you. He's done wonderfully on these cases before. It's honestly just a matter of filing the lawsuit and waiting. If he's in jail because the cops can prove that he was the one who put your life in danger with that fire, then there's almost going to be a guaranteed win for you."

"How would I pay for a lawyer, Jesse?" I laughed a little. "The shop is thriving, sure, but we're still young and have a lot of bills, especially after the fire."

"I can pay for the lawyer's fees," Jesse replied quietly.

I raised an eyebrow.

"How?" The question came out of my mouth before I could stop it.

Jesse paused a moment and then let out a deep sigh.

"Jade, there's something I've been meaning to tell you, but I haven't been quite sure how to say it," he started. "This isn't just a ranch I worked on as a teen or where I grew up." He cleared his throat. "My family owns the ranch." He shifted a little in his seat.

It took me a second to process this. Then I started looking around at the actual mansion around us. Then, I nearly choked on my pizza.

In my mind, I had pictured – from what Jesse had told me in the past – that the owners were nice people who appreciated the good work Jesse had done for them through the years. Naively, I assumed they allowed him into their home to even fix food if he wanted.

"This ... all of this ... belongs to *your* family?"

"Yes," he nodded.

"Wow."

"Jade, I—" He tried again. "Jade, over the time we've lived together already, I have become a different man. For the better. My father says I picked a line of work that left me feeling down and gloomy. Perhaps that's true. But with you at my side, the world doesn't seem so bad or so depressing."

I couldn't help a small blush that started on my cheeks as he said this.

"I can't even begin to describe what I owe to you. Using my family's wealth to pay for your hospital bills or to get you a lawyer... it's the least I can do after how much kindness you've shown me. And, for that reason, I'd like to introduce you to my parents tonight when they get back from town."

I felt my jaw go a little slack. My heart beat so fast, and I wasn't sure, but it felt like I was floating.

"But I want to introduce you to them not as my girlfriend," he continued as he pulled something out of his pocket. "Jade Santana, I'd like to introduce you to my parents as the soon-to-be Jade *Delaney*. Will you marry me?"

He opened the little box to show a ruby ring sparkling brilliantly in the light shining in from one of the large windows.

I let out a gasp. It was beautiful. A circle-cut ruby sat nestled in a band of rose gold, which complemented the ruby enough to almost let the band disappear. To either side of the ruby was a small, clear diamond. The ring must have been worth a fortune... but then again, he had just said he was wealthy.

I wondered how long he had been sitting on this, briefly, before nodding my head.

"I would be honored to become Mrs. Delaney," I said.

Jesse slid the ring onto my finger. It fit like a glove, which was intriguing since I had never worn rings before. Didn't even own one. How in the world had he gotten my ring size?

"I'm glad to hear it," he said as he embraced me. "I don't want to go back to living my life without you, Jade. Thank you."

He gently kissed me. If I hadn't known before, I was now even more certain that I was madly in love with this man. Not only was he so very handsome, but he was kind and compassionate, and he was my superhero. I never imagined I could be so in love.

With the success of the store and now this, life couldn't get any better. I'd have to let Maria know and thank her. It was her idea that had brought us together.

I looked at Jesse.

"We should tell Maria," I said. "She was the one who suggested we buy a store together. She should be the first to find out that we're engaged."

The word felt surreal on my tongue and I thought my face might break from how happy I felt.

"And my parents since I think I hear them driving up," he said. "And you should let your parents know, too. I wouldn't want them to hear it from social media."

I nodded.

With that, the long list of calls soon began. But I couldn't stop smiling.

The End.

Do you like FREEBIE Romance books?
Sign up for my newsletter and get
Grumpy Billionaire Cowboy
An Opposites Attract, Stuck Together Romance
for free!

I wanted the city life. I never thought I'd be chasing horses ... or the ex-Navy seal.

I left my high-powered job in NYC and returned home to help Mom – temporarily. My goal was to get back to the city and back to my career.

But then, who's standing in the lobby, but Zeke, an old friend, ex-Navy Seal, now doing cowboy things. He's changed ... and fills those jeans in all the right places. Rugged and a rock-hard body I want to touch.

Yet the more I try to talk to him, the grumpier he seems. I wonder if he's holding a grudge from when I left years ago. Funny thing is, this man is drawing me closer to him with each rejection.

I'm determined to get him alone. I just never expected to get stuck with him in a rainstorm...

Sign Up Now!
https://dl.bookfunnel.com/j826080it

Printed in Great Britain
by Amazon